# riviera terminus

GEORGE CAVENDISH

Order this book online at www.trafford.com
or email orders@trafford.com

Photography by Christian Wheatley.

Most Trafford titles are also available at major online book retailers.



Printed in Victoria, BC, Canada.

ISBN: 978-1-4251-8754-5 (sc)
ISBN: 978-1-4251-8755-2 (e)

*Our mission is to efficiently provide the world's finest, most comprehensive book publishing service, enabling every author to experience success. To find out how to publish your book, your way, and have it available worldwide, visit us online at www.trafford.com*

*Trafford revised 6/2/2010*

www.trafford.com

North America & International
toll-free: 1 888 232 4444 (USA & Canada)
phone: 250 383 6864 • fax: 812 355 4082

# Author Biographical Note

GEORGE CAVENDISH, son of a British army officer, spent his childhood in the Far East, notably India, Malaya and Hong Kong. Graduating from Oxford with a degree in Politics, Philosophy and Economics in 1974 he worked for 30 years in several international banks in Spain, Gibraltar, the City, France and Monaco. He lives on the French Riviera with his wife and children, now dedicating his time to reading, writing and various other fields of enjoyment and edification such as wine, opera and travel.

*The key to success is sincerity.*
*Once you've learnt to fake that you've got it made.*

*Groucho Marx.*

# Table of Contents

## **acknowledgement** (and disclaimer!)

%

THE AUTHOR WOULD LIKE TO THANK anyone who contributed in any way, voluntarily or involuntarily, to the writing of this book and confirm that any resemblances of characters in the story to real persons are purely coincidental!

Particular thanks to Lee Child who read the manuscript, liked it and encouraged me to write the book. Likewise to the Chairman of Foyles Bookshop, Christopher Foyle.

# VUK

A TRULY MAGNIFICENT COUNTRY. Everything the most enthusiastic writer of travel brochures could dream of. Bold mountains covered with rich and varied vegetation, a sniff of the north; sandy beaches and creeks, a distinct smell of the south. Clear streams and cascading rivers endlessly rinsing the moss covered granite, wildlife prospering and multiplying in this Garden of Eden which western progress had failed to infiltrate. A handsome native race descending from a rich mixture of blood imported from the east and the west, the north and the south.

But the soil of Yugoslavia was soaked in this blood. Centuries of ethnic and religious conflict had done nothing to bring peace or a lasting agreement. Milosovic's solution for ensuring a greater Serbia had left Bosnia in ruins, thousands of families in despair. Missing children, missing fathers, missing mothers, homes pillaged and destroyed, daughters raped and beaten to death.

Nor had it finished. The man who strode like a panther across the garage floor in Avar knew it hadn't finished. His intelligence and ruthlessness matched his size and strength. His huge, powerful figure seemed indestructible, an inevitable survivor of the years of slaughter. None could get the better of this man, this 120kg. Colossus of muscle with the most brutal reputation for ethnic cleansing in Bosnia. A medieval, apocalyptic figure emerging from the slough of Yugoslavia's despond.

He knew it hadn't finished. He knew that whatever agreement the U.N. might find, Serbia's pathological quest for supremacy would spill over again to neighbouring republics, Macedonia, Montenegro and Kosovo. The Krajina conflict in Croatia would also flare up yet again. So the whole thing would go on and on.

Time to get out. Even he was sick of bloodletting. It wasn't so much that he was sick, he was bored. Killing and torturing left him with the same feeling of blandness as a junior clerk who's spent five years licking stamps in the town hall.

Time to get out. And as he looked at the two naked men strapped together in the middle of the concrete floor, he knew also that the time was right.

Vuk studied them disinterestedly, knowing he would obtain what he wanted. He knew everything. How could people be so naive, so stupid, and so apparently unconscious of their own safety, as to imagine they could deceive him? He, the man who pulled all the paramilitary strings, he who had connections going back to boyhood with the apparatchiks within all the main ministries, he who had had the wit and foresight to amass hard cash from narcotics and arms dealing.

These pathetic, snivelling amateurs who had been paid - he'd paid them 50% in advance to get his cash across the border into Bulgaria - had betrayed him. They'd never taken it. They'd come back with cuts and bruises, one of them with a bullet in his leg. Ambushed of course. Victims of a tip-off. But Vuk knew there was no tip-off, no way. Thomas, his right hand man, whom he'd saved from Bosnian guerrillas, who'd given a thousand examples of his unswerving loyalty, was the only other person in the world who knew about the cash.

A vein began to stand out on Vuk's right temple. All of a sudden, he felt that rush of uncontrollable rage which came whenever his interests were threatened. Nobody ever took anything from Vuk Racik.

"Thomas, before we talk to this scum, show them what they need to avoid any misunderstanding."

Thomas uncoiled from a plastic chair in the corner of the garage. A swarthy man, slender, with dark hair receding from what could have been a pleasant face had it not been for his eyes. Dark pools of venom. Calm but psychotic.

He reached across to the ramp where an old Skoda sat in a state of half-hearted repair and picked up a thick cable hanging from the front. He studied it, let some two metres slack down by his feet and cut through it with a giant pair of secateurs.

The two men stared in horror as Thomas approached, casually swinging the cable. They forgot their humiliation, their nakedness, the fact that they were bound together face to face, each man's genitals crushed into the other's.

Thomas looked at them inquisitively, as if waiting for them to speak. But he knew they were too paralysed with fear. One of them could just mouth the word "please" but his jaw started trembling and his tongue was so dry and swollen that he could no longer make the effort.

The cable cut deeply into the back and buttocks of Mr Please and his screams echoed through the empty garage. The other man started crying. Vuk smoked a cigarette as he looked out of the greasy windows at the dawn light.

"Mother fucker, mother fucker," growled Thomas in time to his beating. Sweat began to break out on his temples.

"Stop. Don't kill him. Give the other one his share," said Vuk.

Mr Please's head fell onto his companion's shoulder and emitted a terrible wailing. Thomas held up a mirror so the other man could see what was left of his back. The flesh was stripped away, exposing a butcher's carcass.

"It's here, it's here," he whispered.

"And where is here?" asked Vuk, flicking his cigarette into the man's face, trembling with that manic rage which got worse the more he witnessed the terror and agony he was inflicting.

"In the floor." The man's eyes were beginning to bulge.

"What the fuck do you mean in the floor?"

"We've cemented it over."

Vuk relaxed and looked at Thomas with a smile. This was simpler than he had imagined. He'd tracked down the men to this Croatian village where presumably they had thought they could hide and establish new identities – at a safe distance from the Serbian maelstrom and his own paramilitary troops. But he'd never imagined the cash would be with them. One man's stupidity was another man's luck.

"Thomas, leave him intact for the moment. He's got some work to do. And if he doesn't dig in the right place, cut his balls off and give them to the other one to eat."

"They're probably too small to be able to get your teeth into," replied Thomas. He cut away the bloody rope attaching the two men and smashed his fist into Mr Please's snot covered face. "That's put him out of his misery for a while. Get to work, worm."

Pickaxe and shovel lay in a wheelbarrow across to the left of the garage entrance. Mr Please's partner walked stiffly across the cold concrete floor, trying not to slip in the mess of dirty oil and congealing blood.

///

Half an hour later Vuk and Thomas were in a Mercedes on the way to Blusj on the coast of Croatia. One hour later they were heading southwest in a fisherman's boat. They felt good. In two days they would be in the south of France.

The water lapped against the wooden bow of the vessel as the sun rose behind them and Vuk trailed a long muscular arm over the side. Apart from the sound of the engine which was no more than a subdued thumping from the back, the silence and emptiness of the calm sea made a stark contrast to the deafening roar of war which they had left behind. Even these two savage brutal men felt the din and chaos which they carried in their heads slowly dilute and something akin to peacefulness begin to overwhelm.

But not for long. Vuk snapped out of his ephemeral drowsiness, which he considered a sign of weakness, by twisting open the top of a bottle of vodka and pulling out some salted fish from his jacket pocket. He thought about the two dead men he had left in the garage and chuckled. He looked over at Thomas who was cleaning his nails with a knife.

"Hey Thomas. You sure scared the shit out of those guys. I reckon they would have died anyway. Maybe we should have just left them, why waste two bullets?"

Thomas, never talkative, nodded and continued with his nails. Vuk cast his mind back to the war and the video he had organised at Srebrenica. He had enjoyed that. He had trucked prisoners from Srebrenica to Treskavika mountain and executed them, the video showing no more than his shadow over the corpses.

Trucking prisoners from Srebrenica to Treskavica Mountain had meant driving over treacherous mountain roads for 10 hours (320 kilometers round trip) into the worst fighting in Bosnia, complete with heavy artillery duels. Vuk was not mad but he was diabolically ruthless and vindictive. This had been his punishment for the recent Muslim advance and their gory attack on three of his men patrolling east of Srebrenica. They had slit the throats of each of the soldiers and piled their bodies in the middle of the road to confront the next Serb jeep heading west.

He could visualise the headlines following the discovery of the men he had executed:

*The New York Times* : "Bosnia agonizes over release of massacre video.... deaths of Muslims from Srebrenica shown on TV......................."

The *Reuters* dispatch: "Bosnian television has aired a video of a massacre committed by Serbs in Srebrenica, Bosnia-Herzegovina. But will the people responsible for the atrocity be punished.................?"

*The Independant* "The video, shot by a member of the group, shows six emaciated men being removed from a canvas covered military truck driven from Srebrenica to Treskavica, a mountain in territory south of Sarajevo........................."

*The Washington Post* : "A sickening video of Serb paramilitary soldiers in the act of murdering six Bosnian Muslim youths near Srebrenica sobered Serbia on Thursday..............The graphic film was shot near the town whose name now recalls the worst massacre in Europe since World War Two............"

In fact, in the summer of 1995, Treskavica Mountain was not Serbian-held. Muslim extremist armies were fighting Bosnian Serb troops for control of the Mountain, with daily battles, including mutual bombardment. This was reported at the time by various media sources, including the New York Times which stated that a force of about 130,000 [Muslim] soldiers had more than held its own against the [Bosnian] Serbs over the past year. It had taken strategic high ground, most recently Treskavica Mountain south of Sarajevo, and resisted against all odds in the isolated western enclave of Bihac.

So how would the Western world explain the execution on enemy held territory? And how would the Bosnian Muslims react when they discovered what had happened? Execution of their men right under their noses.

Man, they were going to be pulling their hair out. They would know it was him of course but they would never admit it. Vuk was supposed to have been hounded into a corner somewhere in Croatia. It simply wouldn't do to have the word out that he was alive and kicking. Kicking hard.

Vuk looked out towards the sea on his right and wondered why there were no dolphins following the boat. Shit. Every time he was supposed to see dolphins the bastards didn't show up.

# Author's note

SORRY ABOUT THAT. However, it's pretty much how it happened. I know because I read the report. Nevertheless I'm a bit shocked when I read back those first pages.

This is a strange tale but it had to be told. According to the author, anyway. There are a lot of rather delicate facts and sensitive bits of information which have had to be blurred slightly, for example, by leaving the exact moment in which all this happened a bit vague and mixing up some of the true chronology of events. It's obviously sometime in the 1990's and the reader who knows a bit about the civil war in Yugoslavia will probably deduce accurately the exact year.

There is also a partial insight into the workings of the financial system, and how normal "nice" people working in it can easily be led astray and start laundering. Laundering money, that is. Normal nice people are still human beings (that is some observation) and as such are greedy. They all want more and if there's a quick way of getting more without getting into trouble they will pursue it, usually pretending to themselves, of course, that they're not really doing anything wrong.

To get back to Yugoslavia: we've forgotten most of what happened, haven't we? Between what happened back in that country in the 1990's, which is related to this story even though the story didn't take place there, and now . . . well! Who gives a damn now about Milosevic? At the time, the Yugoslavian civil war was just across the border from Italy so when we had nothing else to worry about it seemed pretty damned close. We all, as educated adults, started mumbling about the Balkans powder-keg, about what history had already taught us when an unfortunate arch-duke was assassinated in Sarajevo, about a third world war with Russia, the Arab world and the West, all at loggerheads.

But now we've got Al Qaida, which has started bringing horror off our television screens and onto our streets and even our doorsteps.

But all of this is beside the point. I just wanted to place the story in its true historical context because it's interesting how the consequences of historical events of the size and importance of the Yugoslavian civil war are not just geo-political but personal and individual. One way or another, the ramifications spill over the borders and seep into the lives of people who probably don't know the difference between Bosnia-Herzegovina and mad cow disease.

The point is not a profound one and indeed I would be incapable of making one, but it really struck me like a slap in the face when I became acquainted, both as actor/observer and raconteur, with the events in this story.

Not many people know much about the ten years or so when peace and cohabitation in Yugoslavia turned into turmoil. It was all so complicated. How about this for a quote? "The key for understanding the roots of the crisis lies in serious and unsolved internal national, religious, economic, social and political problems that, in various forms, and with variable intensity, had smoldered all the time during the seven decades of existence of this multi-national and multi-confessional community of the south Slav peoples".

When I decided, after many years of reflection, to put this story down on paper and, I must repeat, many years after it happened, to make sure the authorities and other interested parties had lost interest, I did some basic reading about the civil war because, as you will see, one of the nasty Serb warlords, Vuk Racik, who got out in time, is a central character. I just couldn't begin to understand how people this barbaric could exist. I thought all the inhuman fascist bastards had been got rid of after the Second World War. That's forgetting the odd Stalin, Pol Pot, Idi Amin, Ayatollah, Pinochet . . . but then they were all so far away. Jesus, I went on holiday in Yugoslavia only a few years before it went berserk.

Potted history lessons are not my forte so I won't regurgitate all the stuff I learned about Yugoslavia's unwieldy constitutional arrangements sowing the seeds of federal implosion, about the economic imbalance between North & South leading all the republics to compete jealously with each other, about Tito's death precipitating the birth of radical Serb nationalism, about the Berlin wall coming down and spelling the end of Communism (which, whatever its imperfections, did more or less glue together the Yugoslavian republics).........and of course we all know what happened under Milosevic and what his psychopathic colleague Karadjic did to the Bosnian Muslims.

Eventually Serbian forces defied the UN completely and overran two "safe areas", Srebrenica and Zeja. Up to 8,000 Muslims were murdered. You will get to know one of the murderers, Vuk Racik, better in this story. In fact shortly before NATO had reacted with an unprecedented series of air strikes against the Bosnian Serbs and peace at last began to be negotiated in Bosnia, he left the country. Our story picks up from there.

One thing I want to make clear before starting the story, because the above already seems slanted against the Serbs: it wasn't just the Serbs, you know. Everyone was having a go at atrocities, revenge and counter-revenge. The Serbs seemed particularly barbaric because they had the likes of Milosevic, Karadzik and Mladic, encouraging and condoning and whipping them up into a frenzy with propaganda and so on. I guess what distinguished them was the ethnic cleansing element which we all thought we'd seen the last of with Hitler.

Anyway, all of this is tangential at best and irrelevant at worst, as far as my story is concerned I mean. My broad and woolly conclusion is that there are obviously not more nasty Serbs than nasty Albanians or Muslim Bosnians or Englishmen for that matter. Or Germans. Bung the wrong bloke in at the top and you move from peace to war in no time at all. There are always a few murderous and manipulative bastards ready and able to stir up that latent barbarity lurking somewhere in the inner recesses of us decent, loving, civilized and law-abiding citizens. *N'est-ce pas?*

I reckon we can all metamorphose into Frankensteins and then switch back to "normal", wondering how on earth we could have done what we did and then wiping it off our memory altogether.

Enough. I'm going to tell you the story.

# LUCAS

VUK RACIK had nothing to do with Lucas Watt. Yet. Lucas was blissfully ignorant of Vuk's existence, let alone his imminent arrival on the Côte d'Azur. He would have remained both ignorant and indifferent had bad luck and cruel destiny not cast him upon his path. He had no idea, this greedy, complacent but likeable man, that his easy, enjoyable life was going to take a nasty turn.

As he stood on the terrace of the "Ruban Bleu" bar-restaurant, he looked out to sea and considered that the Côte d'Azur was at its best. The bay of Juan-les-Pins was sparkling, unclad female youth abounded despite the early season, a waft of garlic, scampi, rouget, vinaigrette and suntan lotion gently assailed the nostrils. A light breeze rolled in from the Iles des Lérins opposite and, as Lucas reflected, everyone deserved a dose of all this. At some time in his life. The nuance was, this was his life. He chuckled to himself. The second seven o'clock beer flowed down his throat, accentuating his complacency.

It was the British colonials who had invented the ritual, the satisfaction of a rosy, alcoholic tint to be added to the magic of sun-bleached foreign climes. Twelve years in the South of France. Better than the underground, the city with its jostling wine-bars, the fetish of real estate investment, the scramble for theatre tickets. And, of course, the weather.

Sod the weather. There was some French actor/crooner (Serge Reggiani?) who sung about Venice not being in Italy; metaphorically it was in your heart and in your, UGH, in your stomach. You know, the sun shines inside if you are at peace with yourself. If you're not at peace with yourself, well, if the sun is shining it just makes you feel even worse. You have every right to be miserable if it's bad weather. But if you feel bad when the sun is out then you've got a problem.

Lucas indulged in his usual jovial introspection. Okay, he'd messed up his private life, but then who hadn't? Life was all about choice, intelligent choice based on objective facts – such as sparkling sea and culinary wafts, nubile creatures cavorting on the sandy beaches, money and .... money. Maybe.

Never lapse into doubt. Doubt about one's life, about cosmic crap, about casualties left behind in the wake of one's "tumultuous" private life – *le passé ne compte pas. C'est le présent. Même pas l'avenir*

The waiter interrupted his meandering thoughts. Another beer? No, no thanks, two was enough. Like fuck it was enough. He could go on knocking it back 'till the cows came home. But keep up the pretence, to himself and those at large. He was reasonable, a bank manager who assumed his responsibilities and permitted himself reasonable relaxation. The waiter didn't know he was on his way to a cocktail party, doubtless followed by dinner with his brother.

Or maybe he did know. That was one of the things about France, there was a sort of tacit empathy with the way others ran their lives. Excess was gallant, carefree, "insouciant". But professional image counted. You couldn't be, openly, a bank manager and an alcoholic. Come to think of it, maybe you could. Mitterand got away with lodging his illegitimate daughter plus mistress in the Palais de Versailles – or wherever. Maybe he'd have that third beer after all.

*"Monsieur, vous m'avez convaincu. Allez. Encore une autre. Mais on s'arrêtera là, d'accord?"*

*"Bien sûr, Monsieur. Tout de suite."*

Lucas' third beer appeared within a minute, staring at him neutrally from the centre of the table.

Shit. Couldn't go on hiding this for much longer. *Vieux beau*, that's what he was. He turned to look at his reflection in the bar's window. Looked okay. He patted his hair. Getting thin at the front. Funny how the less hair you had, the more time it took to coax it into place.

Lucas' latent alcoholism was kept in check by morning tennis, daily swims from May to October and a job which required an active intelligence. Nevertheless he'd accepted that he was at least to some extent dependent on drink but his natural exuberance and irreverence prevented him from taking the problem seriously.

He sipped his beer, lit a cigarette and pulled a brochure he had found in the doctor's surgery out of his briefcase. He pondered with amusement the facetious comments he had pencilled in the margin.

ALCOHOLISM

*It is estimated that 5% to 10% of the adult population in the US is afflicted with alcoholism.* **Yeah, well I live in France don't I?**

*It is more prevalent among men than women, although alcohol abuse among women is on the increase.* **Good, I won't have to drink on my own any more**

*Alcoholism often goes undiagnosed as most alcoholics deny the extent of their usage of alcohol* **No I don't**

*Work, interpersonal relationships and almost all areas of life are affected by their drinking.* **Pleasantly so**

*Physical and emotional abuse is not uncommon in alcoholic families.* **I only indulge in self abuse**

SYMPTOMS

- *Low tolerance for anxiety. .......***Oh yes Doctor, I'm riddled with angst you know, I mean where exactly do I fit into the universe ? I do worry about that**
- *Impaired social functioning......***give me a break, what the fuck does that mean?**
- *Slurred speech .............***Wozzat ?**
- *Lack of coordination.......***Ever seen me play tennis when I'm pissed?**
- *Insomnia; nightmares.........* **Now I come to think of it I did dream about eating a huge marshmallow the other night. When I woke up my pillow had gone**
- *Hangovers, and absences from school and work........***I don't get hangovers any more, nothing a nice cold beer can't sort out**
- *Delirium tremens (tremors, hallucinations, confusion, sweating, rapid heartbeat)..........***The only time I get that is when I can't get a drink**
- *Congestive heart failure (shortness of breath, swelling of feet)...........***The only regular swelling I get ain't in my feet, I can tell you**

Lucas stubbed out his cigarette and allowed his mind to stray on to his work. He'd left the UK clearing bank "syndrome" as he called it, when he married Martine who wanted to live in France. His French was perfect and a heavily influential client/friend introduced him to Geneva based Banque Helvas. They wanted to open offices in the South of France but were reticent about Monaco. One of the senior partners had lost the bank a fortune by buying real estate at the wrong price in Avenue Princess Grace. So Monte-Carlo was out and Nice was in. And Lucas was in too, manager designate at the age of thirty.

Four years later Martine was out. He still felt bad about that. The divorce had been messy. Nothing to do with alcohol of course. Just his rampant sexuality and uncontrollable urge to seduce had led to one affair too many and Martine, although tolerant by nature, realised things were not going to get better. My God she'd negotiated a good package though. It was that fucking lawyer who'd made her so acrimonious and vindictive....and greedy. The longer he tried to reduce the alimony the more his salary increased and his career flourished, pushing Martine to new extremes of exigency.

But my God, it was good working for the Swiss. Not all the Swiss of course, in fact he had strong negative opinions about the Swiss banks in general but not about the one he worked for. A thoroughbred. Old money, in need of a young mind. He'd taken a year to get the bank open. The French administration was a lumbering, complacent giant. Bureaucracy emanating from the Ministry of Finance and the Bank of France drove him to distraction. But he did it. He got the licence, agreed on FRF 75 million capitalisation and signed a nine year lease for the premises. Then he bought the freehold.

The offices were on the fifth and last floor of a 19th century building on the Avenue de Verdun. They overlooked the Prince Albert gardens and the sea and sat above Lacoste, Luis Vuitton, Hermès and a number of other chic boutiques. Discreet luxury, nothing flashy. 250m$^2$ divided into reception, vault and five offices. His was the biggest, 35m$^2$ of carpeted space, greys and blues, a real Gauguin on the wall from the Geneva collection. A large mahogany desk and built in wooden cabinets. In the corner were two leather armchairs, modern, and a sofa. Anyone felt good sitting there. You couldn't help it.

A decanter of fine Glenmorangie and crystal glasses gleamed on a small trolley. He kept the J.B. for himself. Never before 4pm though, when he sat down with Jérôme, his assistant. Except when there was stress, of course, when he poured himself calming shots from 11a;m. But that was an exception.

You had to hand it to the partners in Geneva. They'd got it right. This was no casual endeavour. Not like Barclays opening a branch in Chatham High Street. This branch was there to serve the wealthy, very wealthy, clients of Banque Helvas in Geneva who lived on the Côte d'Azur. There were at least a hundred of them. They needed cash, they needed safety deposit boxes, they needed advice. They needed Lucas. And Lucas had his own very strong and very good ideas about private banking. Never industrialise, keep it very personal, build on the clients' real needs, don't ever try and impose ready made solutions and don't sell products..... sell a service.

A typical conversation between Lucas and a client would go:

*" Good morning Lucas, how are you fixed for Monday afternoon? Fancy a game of golf?"*

*" It would be an honour and a pleasure sir. Give me a chance to talk about those put options we've been selling on your behalf. I think we should stop for the moment while you are still ahead of the game, the market can go down too much with the Asian slump. The premiums are tempting but the risk is not."*

*" Whatever you say Lucas old boy. I never made a loss by taking a profit. Do as you think best now and then we can talk about something else on the golf course."*

His clients' Swiss bank accounts and investment portfolio statements were sent, initially by fax, now over the bank's intranet system and directly onto Lucas' screen. No names, just codes and numbers. The system was parallel to and ran independently of his local bank accounts.

So the clients thought it was great. And it was. No need to risk telephone calls to Switzerland, no need to take a plane to see a portfolio manager. Everything was served up and discussed by Lucas. Right there, a few kilometres from their luxury homes on the Cap Ferrat, Cap d'Antibes, Beausoleil, Villefranche, Mougins and Cannes.

And Lucas was not a fool. He did his job well. So did Jérôme. What Banque Helvas didn't know was that they earned more than their salaries. Far more.

%

As Lucas sat absorbed in his global contemplation of life in general and his in particular, about nine hundred kilometres away Vuk sat on the prow of the fishing boat, watching the Italian coastline approach from the horizon. He drained the last of his drink, an inch or two of neat vodka, and threw the empty bottle in a high arc into the sea. He wiped his wide, stubbly jaw, farted, and lay back against the coiled ropes on the deck.

In a weird pastiche of involuntary imitation, Lucas drained his beer, put his glass on the table, stretched, let a bit of middle aged flatulence out of his system and straightened his tie as he looked at the horizon. A small and ominously black cloud could just be seen to the East. Nothing close enough to spoil the balmy perfection of the evening. He got up, somewhat heavily, and walked to his car.

# GEORGE

AT ABOUT THE SAME TIME that Vuk Racik and Thomas were chugging out of the fishing village of Blusj in a south westerly direction, sniffing appreciatively the fresh, salty air, London was undergoing a vague semblance of dawn breaking. The mist that had settled in the city throughout the spring night was reluctantly peeling back, like a dirty, wet bandage. The silence was only disturbed by the occasional passing throb of a taxi's diesel and the streets were empty. Nobody stirred. The megalopolis was still asleep.

Rylett Road, one of the streets situated in the area between Fulham and Chelsea, parallel to Gunters Grove, was as silent and empty as the rest of London. But a light shone from a second floor window catching, bizarrely, the tailend of some unwanted rodent nightlife which scurried, stopped, looked around with the wariness and assurance of a loner, and then scaled a wall and disappeared.

The flat was well kept and the drone of television news could just be heard from outside. A report on Serbia was being introduced. As the location report cut to a video of the shooting of six pathetic young men all of whom were obviously too tired and ill to care, the BBC commentator's voice quivered with shock and genuine emotion. A shadow was cast across the men as they were lined up. When they collapsed like puppets no longer held up by their strings, the shadow, belonging to the man barking orders to the executioners, moved casually across the inert bodies.

According to the commentator both Muslims and Serbs were appalled but no comment had been made by any Serb leader apart from Mladic: "This is war, what do you expect?"

The shadow spat. The television clicked off, triggered by a remote control held by a pale young man of about thirty two.

He would remember that moment in the coming weeks and ponder, as would his brother, on the hateful tricks which destiny, or the Gods, could play. One minute life was (more or less in his case) under control and the next it veered madly off course with nightmarish consequences. Like his motorbike accident, no way to grope for the remote control and zap off elsewhere.

George Watt lay on his bed, sweating despite the morning chill. He was sweating because of a nightmare and because he felt trapped in the rigid swaddling of plaster: left leg and left arm.

He moved painfully off his bed, struggling with his crutches, swearing as the pain shot through his limbs. Damn it. This time he'd had enough. Enough of lying on his bed, enough of trying to keep clean without wetting the plaster, enough of reading Raymond Chandler, enough of drinking his way through the monotony of lonely days in his flat while the world buzzed outside.

Thank God for Molly. Not even "Thank God", come to think of it. Three years with her and now she was going to leave him. Had left him. She'd tended his wounds, done the shopping, wept copiously and left. No more accidents, no more motorbikes. If he didn't agree, she'd leave. So she left.

He moved, crab-like, across the floor to the bathroom and propped his crutches against the tiled walls. The fluorescent light created hollows in his face, sallowed his complexion and dimmed the youthful gleam in his eyes.

With an effort, he sponged his body, shaved, shampooed and looked at himself in the mirror again. There was a hardening of the jaw, a clarity of purpose, a determination which had been absent only a few minutes before.

Okay. Packing, papers, money. One large case with wheels at the back. It was 5.30 am. He called a taxi for 5.45 a.m., the time it would take to get down the stairs with his crutches and bags and limp out to the street.

///

Despite his discomfort, it felt good to be on the train. Eurostar, Waterloo to Paris, Gare du Nord. God, the French must love arriving in Waterloo, he thought. His spirits lifted. He was moving. This was the beginning of a change. The ideal moment to light up a contemplative cigarette. No fucking smoking. He sat back and relaxed.

He wasn't sure why, but as soon as the train left, he felt as if he was drawing the curtains definitively closed on the UK. He hadn't realised how he had been straining at the leash to escape. For years. At the age of seven he had failed to comprehend the rigid hierarchy of his prep school, the rules, the bullying, the power of the prefects, the uniform.

Lack of comprehension turned to active dislike and rebellion. He had always been in trouble. But he kept his spontaneity. If only he'd known then what he knew now, he would have told them all where to get off. Still, as his parents always said, it had provided a good education. Thank God, he'd persuaded them not to put his name down for Eton. He'd ended up in a minor public school and survived to pass his A-levels.

Since then he'd worked on building sites, and as a coach for foreign students learning English. Finally, he'd set up on his own, buying a powerful motorbike and subcontracting to express delivery firms in London. He stared down at his plastered leg, entrepreneurial debris from his mediocre and now non-existent business. Ah, but the bike, what a bike. Just how fast can you go on two wheels?

He dozed off, only to awake in agony. He could hardly move his leg. Sprawled face down in the corridor was a girl with platform shoes and what must have been a very short skirt, unless it had rolled up unreasonably as she fell. He noted the slender legs and the clumsy shoes. He also noted with a kind of anomalous tenderness her simple white panties. Christ, Molly wore that kind of underwear. His brain cleared and he smiled. The girl smiled back as she stood up excusing herself, speaking French. *"Je ne vous ai pas fait trop mal, Monsieur? Je suis désolée."*

George took a closer look at her. Neat, very neat.

Gamine, yeah, gamine with meshes of straight, shortish, brown hair bouncing across her forehead, the occasional flick of her head to keep it out of her eyes. Brown skirt, tight tee-shirt showing off young breasts and a flat stomach. A huge smile, cheeky sparkling eyes.

He tried to think of something to say in French but could only manage "Don't worry, it was my fault," then remembered, too late *"Je vous en prie, c'était ma faute."* He looked at her regretfully as she continued down the aisle to the next carriage. Blimey, wouldn't mind touching base with that one.

His mind wandered – he'd found the right reply; the girl sat down next to him. He used his wounds to prompt interest and sympathy. They sat closer and could smell each other's breath. Warmth, as he touched her arm. She let her elbow slide down the armrest, nestling against his flank. They looked at each other and, without saying a word, left their seats and walked, her in front, he behind watching her swaying buttocks, towards the end of the wagon. No need to say or know anything. This was primary, this was the essence.

He snapped out of his reverie and rearranged his legs and crutches, rested his broken arm on the table in front of him and looked up just as the train emerged from the tunnel. Within minutes he could see gently rolling countryside, open and vast and scarcely populated. Strange how different and cramped things seemed on the English side of the Channel. Oh, the English, cheerful milkmaids, contented couples sipping tea while watching the village cricket match . . . George allowed himself a few minutes of pastoral whimsicality.

The train hissed along as if on an air-cushion, silent and smooth. This had to be French technology, surely. No way the British could design it. Well, they probably could technically but not culturally. This kind of cushioned comfort would be considered gratuitous and not germane to the basic goal of getting from A to B. Careful George, you've only just crossed the channel and you're getting all anti-British already. Stay objective, don't reject your roots you silly arsehole.

Despite the airtight windows he could smell France.

His idle thoughts kept him awake until the Gare du Nord. As he worked his way painfully along the platform, he suddenly couldn't feel the weight of his suitcase. It seemed to be rolling on its own. He looked down and saw a tanned little hand had wriggled itself round the handle and was taking the strain.

*"Un petit coup de main ne fait pas de mal, hein?"* The girl led him to the taxi rank – forget the metro, you'll never make it. God, French women were . . . what were they? They just seemed sort of delicate and bright and feminine, very feminine. Spontaneous, *légère*? Whatever, they were different. Just like the bread, the coffee, the tobacco, the pastel colours of the Normandy villages. Everything was different.

He was about to formulate a quick list of uncharitable comparisons with English girls when he realised that his little companion had a pen in her hand and was writing her mobile phone number on his plastered arm. She was speaking to him in English. She was going to Nice, too, in July. He could wait a couple of months.

"What's your name?"

"Nath."

"Nat?"

"Nath for Nathalie."

They both laughed.

# BROTHERS

%

AT 8.45PM, while Vuk Racik and Thomas moored in Taranto on the heel of Italy, and picked up a Mercedes which had already been paid for, George arrived at Nice Central. Vuk sat back as Thomas paid off the fisherman. He vowed to fuck every woman he could find when he got to the south of France. French pussy. That's what he needed. Tons of it. He had had his fill of Yugoslavian women. Nice, soft, sweet French pussy. He started getting an erection and squeezed his testicles as he imagined his first lay. Two bitches together, that's what he was going to have and, boy, were they going to get what all bitches wanted.

"Thomas," he shouted, "Get a crate of good champagne. We've got a long drive ahead of us. Don't forget the ice."

%

George sat on the steps at the front of the station, vowing to take his plaster off himself. Ten days early, too bad. His leg stuck out in front of him and he cringed every time a passer-by stepped over it. His bags were assembled next to him and he puffed at his Gauloise. Bit of a tradition that, buying black tobacco when he came to France. He preferred them after a meal but a virtually smokeless journey had left him in need of a stronger shot of nicotine and taste.

The warmth of the evening contrasted pleasantly with the damp cold of London. It had been a long day. Nice station was grubby and busy. It fronted onto Avenue Tiers which was equally grubby and busy, every inch taken up by sandwich bars, squalid hotels, "Babali", the cheapest retailer in France. He noticed a number of North Africans - Moroccans and Algerians, probably. The older ones looked poor, living on the margin of society, but dignified.

The younger ones, adolescents, were different; cocky and colourful, immaculate trainers and neat imitation Nike clothes. They stood around in groups of four or five, clapping each other's hands and laughing. They were quite handsome and seemed defiant, proud, vaguely challenging.

He looked at his watch again. 21.15h. He didn't really mind and he didn't worry. His brother was always late, always trying to cram too much into available time, activities overlapping, speeding. He wondered if he'd changed much over the two years since they'd last seen each other. Probably less than himself.

A gleaming grey Jaguar XJ8 pulled up in front of his plastered leg. The windows were lightly tinted, enhancing the intimate luxury of white leather seats and the discreet walnut veneered dashboard. Lucas got out and looked at him with a smile, his hands on his hips, shaking his head in mock disapproval at his wounded brother. Genuine fraternal pleasure flowed between the two men. George struggled to his feet and they gave each other an uninhibited hug.

"Been in trouble again, eh?"

"Yeah, a wall jumped out at me. I'd rather not go over it now my dearest bro'. What about you?"

"I'll tell you all when we've had a celebratory drink."

Lucas opened the boot and lifted in the suitcase. He opened the passenger door and pulled the seat back so George could swing his rigid leg into the car. He held his crutches against his right shoulder like a bass.

*%*

George and Lucas sat in the latter's apartment with a bottle of whisky on the table and a cloud of smoke permeating the room.

" . . . so the bloke goes into a bank, sees the manager 'cos he's won the lottery, and just before he signs the forms asks the manager – 'Excuse me asking, but would you mind telling me how many times a day you have a bath?'"

George studied the ceiling of Lucas's flat with an expression of polite indulgence on his weary face. How was it that Lucas, a 43 year old bank manager for fuck's sake, still loved telling jokes? And where did he get them from? Was this puerility or a sign of strength............. or weakness............or general *joie de vivre*?

"So the guy looks a bit surprised and asks him why he wanted to know about his washing habits. Answer : 'I know it's all right as long as my account is in credit but if I ever wanted a mortgage I'd have to lick your arse.'"

Lucas collapsed in laughter. George chuckled despite himself. They poured out more whisky and switched to catching up on each other's lives.

"Forget London," said George. "Can you imagine the prospect of spending your whole life there? It's too grim. And I have to admit I'm getting a bit old for delivering parcels on motorbikes. You know what I was earning? £400 a week. Try surviving in London on that. The flat cost me £175 a week and that was a bargain. Then Molly said she'd leave so her contribution was going to dry up and I just thought fuck it. Couldn't even wait to get the plaster off. I just had to move. And here I am."

Lucas looked at his brother with a mixture of exasperation and affection.

"What are you going to do? I mean you can stay here as long as you like but, well, there aren't many jobs on the Côte d'Azur. I suppose you could teach English – to 18 year old French birds of course. Get paid in kind."

George sighed. He knew he had to earn money pretty quickly but his savings would keep him going for a few weeks. He had a self-contained, modest way of enjoying life without consuming much. Lucas envied him this.

"Something to do with restaurants – I don't know, maybe open one."

"Oh great. Crippled, motorbike delivery boy seeks to introduce the French to the delights of English cuisine. Yeah, I think you're onto a good idea, George."

George sighed slightly more heavily. "What about you Lucas, life still a bed of roses, I suppose? Money rolling in, fighting off lascivious French women? King of the Riviera's financial system? *Monsieur parfait?*"

Lucas laughed again. A deep, contagious laugh, not devoid of complacency. "I suppose that's a more or less accurate summary. Bit exaggerated but, yeah, things are going pretty well. I know you think it's all a bit glitzy, but glitz is better than grime, that's what I say."

"So what you say is that there's no grime on the Côte d'Azur, eh?"

Lucas paused a second. A serious look came into his eyes. Serious or troubled, wondered George?

He'd always found that life was far too serious an endeavour with far too many sources of angst for constant levity to be anything but a charade. Maybe a brave charade but a charade all the same. But then when he saw Lucas he couldn't help wondering whether it wasn't perhaps, after all, a game worth playing. As good a solution as any.

# PARTNERS

%

NICE WAS, in Lucas' opinion, one of the most beautiful cities in the world. Sitting on a wide, symmetrically curved bay eight kilometres long (La Baie des Anges, apparently named after the "Anges" sharks which used to frequent it), it fronted the Mediterranean and backed onto green hills dotted with villas and up-market condominiums. His apartment was on Mont Boron, "the" hill to be on. All the hills rose towards mountains and the Arrière Pays which offered skiing in the winter, lakes and spectacular walking country such as the Vallée des Merveilles. The Promenade des Anglais followed the bay and jinked to the left at the end, round to the port where the ferries set off for Corsica, a few hours away.

It was still a city of course, not just a pretty picture like Juan-les-Pins. The centre enjoyed broad, leafy avenues such as Gambetta and Victor Hugo and handsome "bourgeois" buildings. The old part of the town was a labyrinth of little streets crammed with shabby but picturesque Niçois architecture, churches and the famous Cours Saleya. The latter was used as a market place every morning and metamorphosed into the centre of night life from 8.00 pm onwards. But directly tucked behind, to the north east, was Ariane and Trinité, areas largely reserved for the Arab immigrant population. They were dirty, dangerous ghettos, with badly lit streets and ugly "HLMs", the French equivalent of council houses. Trust the French to find a sophisticated euphemism: *"habitations à loyer modéré"* – dwellings at a moderate rent.

It was 6.50am, exactly a week after Vuk Racik and George had set off from their different starting points for the Côte d'Azur. Lucas always took the Promenade des Anglais on his way to the tennis club. The sea was flat in the morning and the sun rose from behind Cap Ferrat to the east, casting a soft, pink light over the cliffs above the port, the fishermen pulling in their nets and the buildings on the front. Sometimes he stopped his car and meditated quietly on the beach for a few minutes. It was all part of his routine, the need for peace, recharging of the batteries after hectic days in the office followed by late nights as he juggled his time between old and new mistresses and the inevitable dinner parties with clients.

This morning he decided not to stop. He turned off the Promenade and drove a couple of kilometres up the Boulevard Gambetta, turning to the left into a smart residential area, Parc Impérial. His club was in the centre of the Parc. Twelve clay courts, six hard courts – "quick" courts as the French called them – and a comfortable club house. The courts were reputed to be the best in the whole of France. Even Roland Garros didn't, apparently, get the love and care provided by Jacquot, the head maintenance man. Lucas nodded to him as he walked in.

*"Vous êtes courageux, Monsieur"*, said Jacquot. *"Vu l'heure, je veux dire."*

*"Je sais, Jacquot, je sais.»*

Lucas's tennis partner was a tall, good-looking man called Eric. Eric Bergé worked out of two offices in Cannes and Cap d'Antibes. His line was real estate, luxury villas in Cannes and Super Cannes, the hills rising above Cannes which dominated the town, the sea, the Iles de Lérins and whole of the Estérel to the west. The Cap d'Antibes was a slightly different market, the top end commanding prices up to £10 million, or even £20 million.

The Cap was for clients looking for some land and the possibility of a house with its "pieds dans l'eau", fronting the water.

Tennis did the men, both heavy drinkers, an immense amount of good. They sweated out their excesses, relaxed, laughed. They built on their natural physical endurance, kept their reactions honed. They shared a litre of Evian mineral water after the game, chatted about women and discussed business.

"Lucas, I've met a guy who seems interesting. Perfect mixture of requirements for both of us. He's rolling in it and wants to buy a villa. I think I'm the only agent he's contacted so far. But he's got a problem and the problem is where you come in with your usual connections."

Lucas' eyes sharpened and he placed his glass back on the table. Eric was a good man. 50% of his "ancillary business", as he called it, came from him. He had incredible contacts. Arab princes, actors, retired expatriate businessmen, singers, songwriters, film directors. The real estate business was a natural conduit for foreign investors.

"I thought you might have something up your sleeve. That's why I let you beat me." Their one-set game had ended in a tie-break which Eric had won 7-5.

"Listen, this guy is some sort of east European businessman. From what he's told me, he's sold up his dealership in Prague, cars I think, together with all his subsidiaries. You know, Budapest, what used to be east Berlin, Warsaw, you name it. He got paid $30 million and he wants to retire, for the moment anyway."

Lucas was instantly absorbed. That kind of money led, automatically, to opportunities for generating commissions. $30 million couldn't lie idle and as soon as it was invested someone in the middle, a broker, a banker, an intermediary, someone like him got a rake-off. The thing was to ensure it didn't involve the classical channels, his bank for example, right at the outset. The trick was to render a service that increased his private income.

"$30 million are not entirely without interest, I'll give you that, Eric."

Eric smiled. Even if Lucas spoke even better French than him, he was still a*"Rosbif"*, master of the understatement.

"He hasn't got it all here, or rather, as I understand it, he's left a chunk in Switzerland and the remaining chunk is here."

"That sounds promising. Hope his French chunk is . . . chunky. I assume it has to be enough to buy a house and live comfortably for a while".

Eric nodded in agreement. "As you say. Now, the whole thing boils down to ..... . well, actually, you've more or less guessed. He wants to settle here, buy a house, get a residence permit, integrate into respectable society and open a bank account. Then I assume he'll just sip beer (and I tell you, he can sip it), get a load of income from his investments and go and fuck everything that moves on the Riviera."

"Sounds like a reasonable sort of fellow to me," said Lucas. "Okay, I get the picture. Where do we start? When do I meet him?"

"Well, you remember that party on Philippe Bohringer's yacht? The one you've invited me to. Ask him along too, or I'll ask him but say that the invite's from you. He'll be grateful for the high society bit and you can have a chat on deck. It'll make you look pretty influential too. This guy's not a kid. He's kind of weird with his accent and all that, but he ain't a kid. No way."

The sun was beginning to rise above the roof of the Nice Lawn Tennis Club. It was time for both of them to go, time for a shit, shave and shampoo as Lucas invariably remarked. They got to their feet, left the usual excessive tip for the pretty little (must get inside her knickers) waitress and walked down to their cars.

"By the way, Eric, you haven't told me how much is involved. What's left over after the chunk in Switzerland?"

Eric was already in his car, slamming the door. He put the key in the ignition and rolled down the electric window. "$16 million. Cash. See you next week."

Even Lucas failed to maintain his usual imperturbable demeanour. His head moved forward and his eyes widened.. "Jesus fucking Christ."

Money gave Lucas something akin to a sexual kick. Or rather, every time he made some, he wanted to have sex. A sort of exaltation. He wondered about the little waitress. Maybe keep her for another day. He couldn't very well screw her in the changing rooms at 7.30h in the morning and maybe she wouldn't agree anyway. Mind you . . . then he thought about his lovely little Chloé, his French girlfriend, who was still in bed at home. She never said no. He'd just have time before going to the bank.

# A NEW FRIEND

GEORGE'S HEART WAS PUMPING, sweat poured down his face, his body was gripped by a paralysing fear. The speedometer showed 80mph as his motorbike flew into the air, performing a slow and ghastly somersault. He saw it detach itself, as if by some tacit accord with him, and float off to the right, exposing its undercarriage and spinning spoked wheels like some giant insect shot down in mid-flight. He saw the grassy bank approaching, saw the young silver beech which folded him in its branches and foliage.

Its trunk bent almost horizontal under the force of the human missile and then sprang gently back, allowing the man whose life it had saved to slide, unconscious, through its branches and land softly at its base.

He sat up, exhausted. The same nightmare, night after night. It was worse than the reality of the accident. He felt weak, gutted. He recalled the soothing rational words of the one psychologist he had consulted about the repetitive bad dreams:

*" Listen," he had said. " Imagine a little boy, called George for example, who is in the middle of a wonderful dream. He's paddling around on his own in the sea imagining he's riding the ocean waves when along comes a giant shark, poised for attack. George tries to move but he can't, he's pinned down by terror and the awful primal eyes of the shark which is slowly moving his tail in the turquoise water. He can't fight off the monster. When he calls out, his mother comes in to see what's wrong.*

*"'It's all right, George,' she says, smoothing his sweaty forehead. 'You had a bad dream, and now you're awake. You're awake and you're safe.'*

*"What you have to remember George is that nightmares are not real and they can't hurt you."*

With this simplistic reassurance George had started to focus more clearly and study the subject. He read about REM, the Rapid Eye Movement phases of the sleep cycle which were at their longest in the early morning hours and during which dreams and nightmares were at their most vivid.

He read about all the likely sources of dreams: stress, illness, death of a loved one, scary movies, fever, medication........motorbike accidents. It didn't seem to matter, they all had to be treated with the same, limited, arsenal of measures.

He had tried establishing a healthy sleep routine, avoiding eating or exercising before bedtime (not that he could exercise much at the moment), avoiding naps during the day, using a nightlight, leaving the door open, rewriting the ending of the encounter with the tree to make it happier and even, to his shame, sleeping with a childhood teddy bear on his bedside table.

He couldn't suppress a smile as he thought of another recommendation: go for a hug from someone close by whom you love. He could imagine Lucas' mixture of shock and horror if he stumbled into his bedroom in the early hours of the morning asking for a cuddle. The humour behind this idea helped him to start functioning again.

It was indeed early, 5.30am. His nightmare always came at about the same time. Lucas wasn't up for his tennis yet and the flat was silent except for the low buzz of the refrigerator installed in the bar. He gave himself five minutes to allow the panic and weakness to subside and then got out of bed and limped gingerly across his bedroom to the window.

He'd taken his plaster off himself three days earlier. The relief was enormous. It was like breaking out of an airless cell. The skin on his leg and arm was grey and lifeless. Worse, both limbs were emaciated. He'd broken his thigh and pulled ligaments in his knee. His wrist had been fractured and his elbow broken in three. The plaster had been on for ten weeks. It was painful, he was diminished and he had to summon all his courage not to weep.

But George had an inner strength which surpassed what his pleasantly modest appearance would suggest. This was a fight and he was going to win it. Lucas had arranged appointments at home with a physiotherapist, taken him for x-rays.

The radiologist pointed to the break and fracture lines, whistled but gave him a reassuring smile. He told him to stick to watching motorbikes on the television. Re-education of his muscles, joints and limbs would take between one and three months – *"Ca dépend de vous, Monsieur."*

After three days, George already felt better. Some of the stiffness had left and he rigorously followed the physiotherapist's instructions. Gentle stretching, bending and lifting exercises. He could cover a few yards without crutches. Yesterday he'd lifted the coffee pot off the bar. Today he was going to go to the beach and wait there while Lucas played tennis.

He stood by the window. Jesus, some view. He thought of Rylett Road, the tiny, scruffy gardens in front of the terraced houses, the paint peeling off his bedroom windows with their worn out sashes, the grey dustbins with their careless lids lying at an angle. The cats, the turd-ridden asphalt.

Peaceful, deep and vast, the Mediterranean stretched out below him. This felt like the first day of creation. He could allow himself the odd cliché when he was alone. He wanted to listen to Cat Stevens, "Morning Has Broken." He smiled. He'd always liked that song, ever since he'd first heard it in the days when he used to sleep with friends in a Ford Transit as they toured Europe and his toe had accidentally jabbed the play button on the cassette player.

Lucas was making stirring noises in the bedroom next door. He could hear him yawning. He moved carefully out of his room to the bar. He was going to make breakfast this morning. Independence. And then he was going to have a good day. He would watch the dawn on the beach, force himself to swim in the still, cold sea, surprise the physiotherapist by his progress and then meet his friend Faruk.

He liked Faruk. He was the only friend he had made so far. Strange guy, obviously a bit traumatised. But then who wouldn't be after what he'd gone through?

Faruk was a Bosnian refugee. And he had a powerful motorbike.

# JOSEF HAVEL

IT WAS TWO DAYS LATER. Thursday morning.

George paddled hesitantly in the bay of Nice, Lucas thrashed around at the tennis club, the city began limbering up for another hot, busy day and Josef Havel lay in bed with an 18 year old Russian prostitute. He couldn't be bothered to screw her again so he pushed her head downwards and put his hands behind the pillow.

She caressed his thighs and lower stomach and turned round on her hands and knees, ensuring that her generous client had a clear view. Josef had to admit that the view was good. Firm round buttocks, slightly whiter than the silky brown thighs, soft trimmed blond pubic hair. Big breasts. He loved big breasts, hanging plumply down as she skilfully rekindled his excitement. She was a good girl but he'd have to get rid of her, of course. No point in taking risks. A whore was a whore.

When he'd fully taken his pleasure, he slapped her bottom and got out of bed. He'd had enough. Until this evening anyway. Perhaps more than enough, his balls were aching. He tucked two five hundred franc notes into her hand with his thick fingers and headed towards the bathroom.

"Clear up and then clear out. Understand, darling?"

The girl pouted and flapped the notes in the air. She looked at him and lay back on the bed with her legs wide apart. "Can't manage any more, big boy? What about tonight?"

"Don't call me – I'll call you." Something in the tone of his voice made her tense. She felt slightly stupid and sat up, clutching the stained sheets against her. Josef could see she wasn't going to bother him again.

The girl gathered her clothes, stripped down the bed and emptied the ashtrays. The bottle of vodka that Josef had first half-finished and then forced her to drink out of while he screwed her lay on its side on the floor. She suddenly felt disgusted and frightened.

Josef was still in the shower by the time she'd finished dressing and tidying up.

She wondered whether to wait to say goodbye and decided against it. As she walked past the bathroom door she heard Josef's mobile phone ring. The shower stopped and she heard him speak roughly, like a beast, in a language she could just understand.

She left the hotel suite and went home. She wanted to wash.

# SOCIETY

LUCAS' XJ8 GLIDED forward with its usual smooth force, and then accelerated out to the A8 motorway, west towards Cannes.

" . . . Yeah, so anyway, this mouse with the cockney accent . . ."

"Oh, I see," said George. "Mice have accents, do they?"

"Yeah, yeah, of course they do. You know that. Think of the days when you were trying to catch them in the East End."

"Go on then." George was glad to be listening to Lucas' banter. It made him relax, feel less nervous about the evening on Bohringer's yacht. He'd never been to a really smart occasion like this. Lucas had lent him a white jacket he couldn't get into any more.

"Well, he's walking down Piccadilly, minding his own business . . ." George stared out of the window of the car at Marina Baie des Anges, a landmark building designed to look like a couple of waves, a berth attached to every apartment. ". . .when some bastard kicks him off the pavement into the middle of the road. Fucking great double-decker bus . . ." The motorway narrowed from four lanes to three and the speed limit signs showed 130 kph instead of 110kph. Lucas accelerated briskly from 140 kph to 170 kph ". . . smashes into him and he's left there gasping with half his innards destroyed."

The exit for Antibes slipped by and Lucas sat back contentedly behind the leather steering wheel. George observed his complacent but lovable brother.

"So he crawls across to the other side, finds a music shop and asks the bloke behind the counter if he's got any mouse organs . . ."

"Is that it?" asked George, trying to sound interested. His mind wandered to Piccadilly and an image of his impressionable adolescent self walking up and down looking at the work of the pavement artists flashed across his mind.

"Hang on. So the bloke behind the counter says he's sorry but he's right out of mouse organs and it was funny he (the mouse) should ask . . ." The car started slowing at the exit to Cannes, and George clung nervously to the handgrip above the door as he saw that their speed remained above 120 kph. "....'Cos another mouse had been in earlier asking for the same thing. 'Oh', says the mouse, 'That must have been Our Monica.'"

"That's terrible, Lucas."

%

Philippe Bohringer's yacht was moored some 500 metres outside the old port of Cannes. As Lucas nipped into a lucky parking space on the Place Mérimée, he and his brother could see two tenders, one ploughing slowly towards the yacht, "M.Y. Arcadia," the other returning. Guests were being ferried out, Lucas explained. They took their turn on the quay. George looked at the port, "Le Suquet," which was the old part of the town directly above, and the islands directly across, Sainte Marguerite and Saint Honorat. Sometimes the Riviera seemed too good to be true. Where was the catch?

M.Y. Arcadia was a prestigious yacht. Its 55 metres length did not make it one of the biggest in the Mediterranean but it was one of the most tastefully fitted and equipped. Bohringer stood smiling on deck as he watched the tenders come and go and welcomed his guests, some 50 odd, individually. Lucas introduced George and they moved forward to the bar.

George discreetly observed his brother who was suavely mingling with the other guests. He was obviously popular and well-known, both with colleagues in the same line as himself and with clients. He made them laugh, seemed to have a confiding comment for everyone, leaning close to his interlocutor's ear, making the latter feel privileged.

There was one man who stood out amongst the guests. Lucas was clearly working his way towards him, step by step, handshake by handshake. George studied him. Impressive. He must have measured 1m95 and was built like a tank. No fat. A round, bearded, Scandinavian looking face set on a thick neck. He was immaculately dressed in a blue silk suit and he would have been distinguished but for a certain coarseness in his features.

George heard his voice booming 10 metres across the crowded deck. Sounded like a bear, he thought – in fact, the man's whole appearance made you think of a bear. A fucking great strong, dangerous bear, George said to himself.

"Lucas? Lucas Watt? Hi, am I pleased to meet you. Eric told me all about you. Seems like you're the best banker on the Côte d'Azur."

Lucas drew him a bit further from the crowd, perhaps slightly embarrassed by the effusiveness.

"You got it. And I know who you are, equally from Eric. He said you were infinitely cleverer than both of us because you're intending to retire before you're 40."

Josef Havel's laugh was loud. He slapped Lucas on the back. "I just got lucky! And you know something Lucas? The harder I worked the luckier I got!"

As they moved out of earshot, George was surprised to be approached by Bohringer.

"George, I'm glad to meet you. I'm a fan of your brother. It's nice to meet someone from his family. How are you finding the Côte d'Azur?"

George liked the man. Obviously sincere. He gave him a straight answer, echoing his thoughts on the quay.

"The catch?" asked Bohringer with surprise. "The catch is just beneath the surface, my friend. Scratch a bit and you'll unearth all sorts of stuff. You see the "Suquet" for example? Right below that you've got a load of bars and pubs. All controlled by the mafia for drug peddling. Nearly all, anyway. A lot of the nightlife establishments here have to pay protection money.

"Then there are the casinos. You've heard about Mouillot, the previous Mayor of Cannes. He's in court for taking bribes, three million francs for granting a licence to the Carlton, God knows how much for the casino licence in the Noga Hilton. There were also one or two strange coincidences when he was in office: building permits would be granted, for a large commercial centre for example, and then the lending bank would withdraw the loan when the project was 90% finished. The builder would have to sell up prematurely at under 50% of the value and the purchaser would turn out to be a subsidiary of the bank. Can you imagine? Then take a look at the yachts. Who owns them? Offshore companies, Panama, Liberia, you name it. But who's behind the companies? There's a lot goes on on the Côte d'Azur which it's better not to know about."

George looked up at the Guernsey flag fluttering gently on the rear mast. Bohringer laughed.

"Don't worry. That's just convenience. Get's round a few V.A.T. problems, legally. I made clean money and I paid my taxes, as much as I had to anyway, and that was more than enough. Did Lucas tell you what I used to do? Made oxygen in the seventies, sold it in special canisters which doctors and asthmatics could carry around in their pockets for emergencies. Then I got into all sorts of ecological stuff, sold up in '92 and took up residence in Monaco. Bit claustrophobic actually, but the only civilized place in the sun which doesn't set off my tax allergy."

Bohringer excused himself, shook hands again, and walked over to say something to his captain. The latter nodded and pulled over one of the crew who reappeared within a couple of minutes with a fresh tray of drinks.

///

By 11pm, George was exhausted. He needed his crutches after all the standing. He'd drunk too much and so had Lucas, who spotted him wilting in a corner of the yacht's bar on his own.

"Time to ease off?"

"It's either that or I'm going to pass out."

Back in the seated comfort of the Jaguar, Lucas recounted his evening. He was elated and the drink had glazed his eyes.

"I tell you, me 'ole mate, I'm onto something really good."

George waited for him to go on. There was something about the money game that irritated him. Bohringer was okay, his was a solid financial edifice built on the manufacture and sale of real merchandise. Lucas' affluence seemed superficial, built on the quasi-illusory need for an intermediary. And he didn't even understand what his intermediary role was. There was something frenetic and greedy about his brother which bothered him.

"Yup, really good. You remember that big bloke? Czech or something. Eric knows him. Well, he is going to be one hell of a big client. Private, for me and then for the bank. That's what I call harmonious. I'm going to play tennis with him and then we're going to sit down with a nice cold beer and talk business."

Lucas was obviously waiting for an appropriate reaction.

"As long as you know what you're doing, Lucas. Looked a bit of a thug to me. Sort of bugger who might send you a few curved balls."

"Bollocks," retorted Lucas.

But the evening had gone flat all of a sudden. They sat in silence until they got back to Lucas' flat. Then they both went to bed. Neither of them wanted to drink any more.

# FARUK

FARUK LIVED on his own in a studio buried in the heart of the Ariane, the poorest, dirtiest, most depressing area of Nice. What must have once been a simple Provençal valley leading down to the sea, flanked by rolling hills covered with pine trees and Mediterranean flora, was now a grim and dusty enclave for the poor, the majority of whom were immigrants from the Maghreb. To the north west, the hills had been eaten away by quarrying and closer to the sea, on the same side, were cemeteries and the town's garbage cremation unit.

At the bottom of the hills were a variety of depots and warehouses scattered amongst the council houses. A layer of dust seemed to cover the entire area, perhaps blown off the quarries. Everything seemed colourless and drab. A motorway connection leading to the A8, west to Marseilles, east to Vintimiglia and Italy, cut a swathe through any attempt that might have been made to form a coherent suburb. At the "smarter" end of the Ariane, closer to the sea and at the top of the Boulevard Pasteur, stood the Pasteur hospital, flanked by Lacassagne, best known for its cancer ward.

It was as if the city authorities had decided to concentrate everything that its citizens preferred not to think about in one place, at the back of Nice, out of sight and out of mind.

Faruk didn't care. He was alive and young and burned with energy. He had survived capture, a concentration camp, two years in Sarajevo. His physical condition was excellent. But buried inside his head and heart were traumas of a different kind. He could slowly blunt the pain but he would never forget the massacre of his parents, the mutilated body of his younger sister. Nor would he forgive the perpetrators. One day he would obtain revenge.

He'd managed to get political asylum in 1993. He'd been lucky, his dossier had been treated at a time when the French, in common with other European nations, were keen to manifest their humanitarianism. He'd found a job in a restaurant, "Le Yacht", on the port of Nice where he worked as a *"plongeur"* in the kitchen, doing the washing up. He'd had an English girlfriend for two years before the girl had returned to England and managed, thanks to their endless conversations and her patient coaching, to attain a remarkably good level of English.

In his free time he tinkered with his motorbike, a Kawasaki 900, and when the weather was fine he would drive to the sea-front, chain his bike to the railings on the Promenade and sit in his favourite spot in front of the Beau Rivage hotel. The sea soothed him, the wind blew the stench of the kitchen out of his lungs and the sun tanned his dark face, which made so many people think he was Moroccan.

He inevitably slipped into the Cours Saleya afterwards, sipped a coffee or, depending on the time of day, ordered a "Leffe", the strong Belgian beer which made him light-headed after one glass.

This agreeable but lonely routine was interrupted one day when he struck up a conversation with a young Englishman. The man had been standing with the aid of crutches looking at his bike and had then crouched painfully to look at the engine. Faruk greeted him.

"Hi, you want to buy my bike?"

George laughed. "No, no way! I nearly killed myself on one of these machines. Just a few months ago. I love looking at them though. Kawasaki 900 huh?"

"Yes," replied Faruk proudly. "Next one is going to be the 1100. What happened? How did you come off your bike?"

George pondered the question. "Well, I've looked at it from every angle and I even have nightmares about the whole thing. But you know what the stupid bloody reason was really? I was tired, I was in a hurry and I lost control at 80m.p.h. That's about 140 k.p.h."

Faruk whistled. "That's crazy. How come you're still here to tell the story?"

"All thanks to a tree believe it or not. Hug a tree every day is what I say. It cushioned me in mid air although I still managed to break everything on the left side: elbow, leg, ribs, you name it."

Faruk looked at him with sympathy. " I think that earns you a coffee. Want one?"

George looked at his watch. "Sure, but I'll have a beer if you don't mind. This is opening time in the U.K. Sparks off this Pavlovian reaction, see?" He let his tongue hang out and panted like a dog. Faruk found this hilarious.

"Hey, if you can be thinking about beer at this time of day I reckon you've got over your motorbike trauma. We'll drink to no more nightmares, OK?"

George felt as if a balm had been lightly poured over his anguished soul. Simple kind words from a simple nice bloke. Maybe that was all that was needed.

Faruk liked the Englishman. George was easy-going, no trace of the unspoken disapproval he felt from the French. He was interesting, curious, a pleasant companion, and they met frequently, Faruk walking slowly next to his limping friend.

After a couple of weeks, when George said he was looking for work, Faruk introduced him to the restaurant manager, Monsieur Charles. The latter needed an English speaker at the bar, and agreed to take him on a trial basis and on two conditions: George had to improve his French, considerably, within a month and he had to get his residence papers sorted out. The former was a challenge and the latter a tiresome but relatively easy formality. George accepted.

And so their friendship deepened.

"Tell me about England, George," said Faruk one day. "I have this weird sort of caricature in my mind: lots of disciplined but eccentric and badly dressed individuals standing patiently in queues, like on another planet."

George considered this oddly accurate perspective. He thought about the detached and insular mentality which had not changed despite the centuries of empire building in far flung corners of the world. He thought about the British communities which had formed in the south of France. Totally unintegrated, hardly speaking a word of French and always moaning about the "frogs." And pretty damn sure of their superiority.

" Not sure it's that much of a caricature actually," he answered. "England **is** a weird place in some ways, but totally mundane in others. Mundane like everywhere can be I guess. At the same time there are pockets of excellence, again like everywhere, and there are one or two exceptional people or things or traditions or bits of countryside which make you sort of proud to be English. But with the weather and all that you can get depressed without even realising it.

"I'm supposed to be English, I am English, but I still don't really understand them which some would say means I don't understand myself..........but that's just a load of pseudo psycho crap.

"When I see the way people live down here, how they behave and talk, I realise something has been missing for the last 30 years of my life. The English can't express emotions properly you see, they have difficulty finding the words because somewhere along the line it's not really approved, it's embarrassing. And when they do loosen up, usually after a few drinks, it doesn't sound right and they tend to go overboard. It comes out wrong, the tone of voice.

"Listen to a French person talking to a child and it's great. Warm, natural. An English person in the same situation and it sounds flat and artificial by comparison. Blimey, a Frenchman can pat a child's bum and say 'Oh you have got lovely little buttocks' and it's totally natural but an Englishman, even a paedophile , could never bring himself to say that. Or if he did he would get locked up for life. Must be the language I suppose. But the language carries the culture so it reflects what the people behind it are like.

"Anyway, all I know is that I feel freer here and a lot is to do with the fact I become another person when I speak French. Try saying 'Darling I love you' and it will never sound so good as 'Chèri je t'aime.' Not that I have anyone to say that to at the moment!"

Faruk repeated both phrases with exaggerated accents and roared with laughter. He loved this sort of conversation. He found it intriguing that both the English and the French could be so self critical.

"That's all very well, but do you actually like the French?"

Another pause for thought. "I find them negative, lazy, hypochondriacal, stubborn, slightly neurotic, highly intellectual, often a pain in the arse. Yes, I do like them! I mean it. Maybe they're lovable *thanks* to all their faults. They're completely open about them."

"What about humour?" Faruk asked. "Do you think the French have a sense of humour? I know the English do. We get Benny Hill on Channel 3, translated into French! "

George was amazed. How could Benny Hill's brand of smut, sexual innuendo, farce and naughty rhymes translate into French for God's sake?

"Mind you Faruk, that kind of backs up one of my theories. I think the French have a terrific sense of humour but it's under-developed in a day to day sense. They could unwind a bit if they tried telling a few more jokes. They are a great audience but they don't really have the joke telling tradition like us. I don't think so anyway. Jokes are essential for us, it's part of everyday life and part of our stoicism. When things get bad we actually try and see the funny side." George thought about Lucas for a moment and then went further back to his parents.

"My dad was in the army and he typified this in some ways. It would be pissing down with rain and he would pull us kids out for a walk because walking in the rain was fun, because it was intrinsically a ridiculous thing to do. And of course there was something tough about it, facing up to the elements and making a joke about it. 'Come on you lazy dogs,' he would say, 'Put your flippers on, we're going to get some exercise, get the blood circulating.' If you did that in France you'd probably get reported for attempted homicide and the children would get about five suppositories rammed up their behinds."

Faruk snorted. Weird indeed. "I thought the Brits didn't even know what suppositories were. I even heard about some unfortunate bloke who got some prescribed and ate the bloody things!"

This didn't surprise George at all. "Well, now things are getting Freudian are they not? The English have an anal complex in my view. An arsehole is something you can only joke about 'cos that's the only way to approach the subject. Far too embarrassing to acknowledge that arseholes might be a serious matter............."

Faruk slapped his leg and bent over double.

"............so they joke about them, whence the whole smutty scatological tradition!"

George felt rather pleased with his spontaneous analysis. Hmmm, to be developed, he might be onto something.

%

Faruk could see that the work at the bar suited George. He started at 9am every morning, cleaned the glasses, arranged the bar stools and beer mats, swept up behind the bar and carried crates of empty bottles to the back of "Le Yacht," stacking them in a courtyard.

The physical work was hard, he could only carry half as much as he would have been able to normally, but as each day went by his strength increased and he learnt the knack of leaning back to take the weight on his stomach. The beer barrels were changed every two days and there was room to roll them out and avoid lifting them. Delivery vans came and went and fresh supplies of liquor and soft drinks had to be neatly placed on the shelving behind and underneath the bar.

The first customers would come in at about 11am. After an hour, the tempo increased and he had to cope with staccato orders from the three waiters throughout the lunch hour until 1.30pm when coffees and "digestifs" had to be prepared. By 2.30pm he was free for the afternoon, having cleared up again, and at 5pm he started his second shift. By midnight he was free. "Le Yacht" closed on Sundays and he had a half day on Wednesdays, as did Faruk.

One evening, about a week into his new post, Faruk invited him to meet some friends in "McMahon's", a Guinness pub with live music until 2a.m. on the Avenue Jean Jaurès.

Faruk introduced him to the small group sitting at a table at the back of the pub: Ahmed, Edouard and Saleh. They were friendly enough and spoke good French. All of them were aged between 25 and 30. A fire burned in their eyes.

George listened and understood enough to catch the horror of their tales of ethnic cleansing, their lost families, their hand to mouth existence as refugees living on their wits and government handouts. Saleh belonged to an organisation called "Justice for Bosnia" and had contributed several pages to an internet website. He gave the address to George, who still understood little or nothing about how it could have happened.

They shook hands and bid farewell when the pub closed. All of them, except Faruk, were slightly drunk. Faruk had said little or nothing all evening. His eyes had stayed expressionless but his face was as hard as granite.

# BALKAN WEBSITE

GEORGE GOT BACK from "MacMahons" at 2.30am. Faruk had taken him back on his Kawasaki. The night air in his face cleared his mind and he let himself quietly into Lucas' flat. A half naked girl flitted out of the bathroom into Lucas' bedroom. He smiled. That was Chloé. What a body. He felt a twinge of jealousy and arousal. Lucas had better hang on to that one he thought, before he became too jowly and thin on top to pull the birds. He would broach this with his brother in the morning.

He looked at the bar and hesitated. Lucas was an influence in more ways than one. Then he poured himself a stiff Bourbon, filled the glass with ice and sat down at Lucas' desk. He switched on his P.C., fingered the button on the internet modem and waited for the screen to light up. He tapped in the address which Saleh had given him and read the somewhat rambling and emotional text.

***JUSTICE FOR BOSNIA. JUSTICE FOR ALL.***

*People have been killing each other in Yugoslavia for hundreds of years. Does that mean it's inevitable? Can you stop it or is ethnic hatred too strong a force?*

*The world must understand that tension in Yugoslavia, the wars and blood, are not just the result of people hating each other like rats in a cage. We believe that Croats, Serbs, Bosnians, Slovenes and Montenegrins can and want to live peacefully together.*

*The torment of Yugoslavia is the result of complex and shifting world and regional power struggles. Yugoslavia has acted too often either as a territory fouled up between different empires – Austro-Hungarian, Ottoman, Holy Roman – or as a buffer zone between the eastern and western world powers which emerged in the 20th century. Conflict is the result more recently of political chaos following the death of Tito, compacted by the economic crisis.*

*Power structures have too often been destabilised in the former Yugoslavia and ethnic nationalism has taken hold in a complicated political mosaic of race, history and religion.*

*What people do not know is that there is a long history of peaceful cohabitation among these religious groups, particularly in Bosnia, where they overlap to the largest extent. And this is despite the legacy of Ottoman rule which created the potential for deep historical resentment of Islam among Christians in the Balkans. That history is there to be manipulated. We see that today, together with its murderous impact. It is the manipulators upon whom the world must focus its attention.*

*Ironically it was the half-Croat, half-Serb Tito fought alongside his communist partisans to unite our poor country. He asserted that the nations of Yugoslavia should be treated equally. Yugoslavia was reborn. Why should it now be dismembered and tortured?*

*Do you remember? Our external borders were open, we travelled abroad, we brought foreign currency back here. We were unique amongst eastern European communist countries. What are we now? A shambles, a nightmare, an inferno of slaughter and corruption. In the name of what? Justice? Correcting the wrongs of history? History was made by our fathers. We are here to avoid their mistakes, not allow a handful of megalomaniacs to exploit it and pour salt into ancient wounds.*

*Ethnic groups used to live together in harmony. How long ago? A few years. Intermarriage was common. Most of us iden-*

*tified ourselves as "Yugoslavs", not Serbs or Croats or Muslims or Slovenes.*

*Do you remember Sarajevo used to be a beautiful city, home to the Olympic games in 1984?*

*Tito's regime was that of a strict father. His control was heavy and equality was not complete, far from it. But he created an entity, a unity. He reorganised and therefore created our republics of Slovenia, Croatia, Bosnia, Hercegovina, Montenegro, Serbia and Macedonia to reflect our different nationalities.*

*Of course we, the Bosnian Muslims, were held as a separate group with no national identity. Did this sow the seeds of today's chaos? Does it matter? We lived in peace. Now we don't.*

*Why? Because when Tito died, the federal government was crippled by disagreements among its various presidential representatives from the different republics. Political leaders thought only of their careers and blamed economic crisis on the supposed treachery of the other republics. From there, one step to ultra-nationalism. Look at the politicians in Croatia and Serbia. Their leaders have spouted propaganda to manipulate the injustices of the past and justify the aggression of today.*

*The tragic impact of so many hundreds of years of bloodshed and confusion is the vast amount of history available for manipulation. Current leaders exploit the past to spread fear and bolster their own power. Political gain at the price of terror and uncertainty. .*

*Greater Serbia was brutally constructed. People who had previously lived side by side in peace were forced into war.*

*What we want to say is the following: given the bloody memories of the past, it is easy to understand how the fire was started. But how do we put it out? This is the question that we, "Justice for*

*Bosnia", pose not only for the victims of Sarajevo and Srebrenica but for everyone in Yugoslavia.*

*We say there are no more villains in Croatia and Serbia than anywhere else in the region, or in the world. But our villains are free. Worse still, they are in power. And while they're in power, 10 million innocent hearts are bleeding.*

*So much chaos and suffering caused by cynical, heartless tyrants and their henchmen is rare, unique even, in Europe. Since the fall of Hitler, it is unimaginable.*

*The tyrants and the henchmen must be brought to justice and eliminated from the political scene. They must be tried and executed. Here are the key names, the mad dogs who must be put down:*

*Slobodan Milosevic**
*Radislar Krstic**
*General Ratko Mladic**
*Radoran Karadzic**
*Tihomir Blaskic**
*Vuk Racik**

*If they are left free, the killing of innocent people will continue. And our children will be ashamed that we did not have the courage to protect them. They will not forgive us.*

George clicked on each name. He knew about Milosevic, the satanic figure behind so much of the evil inflicted in the region. He'd read about Krstic and some of the others. He clicked on the last name and read the following:

***RACIK Vuk.* Single. Born April 15th 1959 in Nice, France. 1.93m. No living kin apart from twin brother (Krazik, whereabouts unknown). Student, University of Belgrade 1979-1983. B.A. 1983 in Social Sciences, Doctorate 1985 Ethnic Studies.***

***Thesis submitted "Convention and Reality Concerning Racial Differences". Languages : Serb, Serbo-Croat, Czech, Russian, English and French. Enrolled in Serbian military police 1986 as Officer Cadet, promoted to Captain 1987. Head of Paramilitary forces in Krajina region 1990 and decorated by President 1993. Promoted to Colonel 1994 and closely involved with Krstic and Mladic in siege of Sarajevo and manoeuvres in Srebenica. Personally responsible for torture and murder of 2,000 citizens and organisation of mass graves. Sent to Kosovo early 1992. Last seen in Croatia. Known to have left Yugoslavia definitively. Probable countries of residence: Italy, Greece, Southern Mediterranean. Any information concerning whereabouts to be reported to U.N. Prosecutor, Mark Harman, The Hague.***

****See "Crimes Against Humanity", www. .....***

George sat back and took a last puff at his cigarette. Wearily, he thought about how he was smoking too much. He remembered that Vuk Racik was the man Faruk's friends had talked about most during the evening. He also remembered that as soon as his name had been mentioned, Faruk had fallen silent.

He went to bed. The clean shaven face with the mop of dark thick hair framing it and which stared indifferently out of the photograph of Vuk Racik on the website haunted him. If the man spoke French, he wasn't going to set up shop in Italy or Greece, was he?

# PROPOSITION

GEORGE WAS STILL ASLEEP when Lucas got up at 6.15h to get ready for his tennis. He left Chloé, the youngest and most easy-going of his string of mistresses, in bed. He looked at her. Was it a good thing this paternal tenderness he felt for her? It was nice spoiling her and cuddling her. She was small and fresh and sweet and clung to him like a limpet in bed, but left him free to run his life and his business affairs. And then he had to admit he felt different when he made love to her, compared to the others. There was a communion between their bodies, the sex was clean somehow, no fantasies, just the warmth of penetration and the intensity of coming, invariably, together.

Careful Lucas, careful. Chloe was 17 years his junior. What would happen when he started putting on weight and losing more of his hair? He'd sworn never to get married again and anyway, what a foul way to tie up a person – a legal contract. Everyone should be free to come and go without getting involved in the law. Unless there were children. Even then . . . his circular thoughts rambled on as he fished a Diet Coke out of the fridge and pulled on his immaculate tennis gear.

He'd been looking forward to this moment. It had been 12 days since the party on M.Y. Arcadia. Josef Havel had been in Paris it seemed, and he, Lucas, had not wanted to follow up too quickly on their conversation. He was, he had to admit, a slightly too energetic businessman, prone lately to taking more and more risks, but he had learnt never to appear impatient. It gave the wrong impression. It was far better that Havel had contacted him – "Hey, Lucas, my friend, what about that game of tennis, or are you scared about losing?"

He slipped out of the flat and was soon driving along his familiar route round the port towards the Promenade des Anglais. He arrived in front of the club just before 7.00am, locked his car and waited, as agreed, outside the main gate. Havel arrived five minutes late in a Mercedes. When he got out of the car, Lucas couldn't help noticing his size and superb physique. He shook hands, already feeling slightly dominated.

"Lucas, you're looking pretty good. What's the secret – wine, women and song, I bet!"

"Wine, women and work, Josef. Some of us have to work to stay alive, you know."

He felt slightly uneasy about his remark. You could never tell what might offend people. Havel released one of his bearish laughs.

They walked up from the road towards the club house, Lucas swinging his racket nonchalantly at his side, trying not to look too dwarfed by Josef. The centre court was in pristine condition as usual and there was nobody to be seen except Jacquot who unlocked the main gates at 6.00a.m. everyday.

On the left were courts 1,2,3, and 4 with the club house and its terrace running across the back of each court. Many a Saturday afternoon had Lucas spent on the terrace, drinking beer, chatting with his friends and watching the local hopefuls. Why not? After all, the club had produced Yannick Noah.

Lucas saluted Jacquot jovially and asked for his permission to use the centre court.

To Lucas' relief, their game was evenly matched, his own mature, solid style enough to ensure a 7-5 win over Havel's size and strength. He felt more confident when they sat down at the far end of the terrace outside the clubhouse and ordered mineral water.

The sweat poured off Lucas as he heaved a satisfied sigh and pulled his chair forward to rest his elbows on the table. They chatted about the game, complimented each other and then Lucas asked his companion to tell him a little more about himself and his requirements. Havel spoke smoothly and succinctly for about five minutes.

"Well, Lucas, that's more or less it", he said as he finished a long and convincing explanation about the sale of his car distributorship. "I'm sure I got out at the right time. My business was apparently one of the few with growing demand and profits in Eastern Europe. The price I got was a one-to-one multiple of last year's turnover, which itself was twice that of the previous year.

"But there's no way the growth will continue like that. No way. So I reckoned 30 million dollars was more than a good deal. Of course, the guys who bought it, real-estate people, had vast amounts of cash. In fact, they wanted to pay 80% in cash – can you imagine? I told them they had to be fucking crazy – there was no way I could justify to the tax vampires that I'd sold up for 6 million dollars."

"So you compromised," said Lucas helpfully.

"You got it, Lucas. Exactly. 14 million above board and 16 million in a fucking suitcase. I paid the capital gains on the 14 million and left the country. Put it into Switzerland. We might talk about switching it to Banque Helvas in Geneva if you manage to help me out with the cash. And there'll be a little something in it for you, Lucas. Don't worry, I know the rules of the game."

Beautiful, thought Lucas. Just plain, fucking beautiful. So he got the private business, put it through the usual channels and Banque Helvas got the official stuff and, doubtless, would give him a decent bonus for such an important new account. He could feel the adrenaline pumping into his brain, but kept outwardly calm.

"Well, Josef, it all looks interesting to me, and I think your idea about putting your Swiss money into Helvas Geneva is a good one. That way we stay in touch and you can do all your Swiss banking through me in Nice."

Josef showed interest. "Oh yeah, how come, Lucas?"

"I'll show you when you come to the bank. It's all electronic now you know, Josef. All you need is a screen, a code and . . . well, me! I'll need a few days to think about the cash, it's a lot."

Havel slapped him so hard on the back that even Lucas' solid frame shuddered. He registered the impact in his mind and a twinge of insecurity crept back, slightly dulling his mounting elation.

They agreed to meet on Friday, two days later.

%

Havel went back to his newly rented room in the Hotel Westminster on the Promenade des Anglais, showered and made a quick telephone call.

"Thomas, where the fuck have you been? You were supposed to call me last night. Get your arse round here."

Half an hour later Thomas let himself into the suite and sat down on a chair by the glass table, which was littered with brochures, a variety of currencies, two passports and a flat leather briefcase. He crossed his legs and waited for Josef. Even he had almost got used to calling him Josef now. It amused him and he preferred it to Vuk anyway, even if it sounded like it belonged to a fucking Yid. He'd never met a Christian called Josef. Just Yids. He'd kept his own first name and his new passport carried the surname Dresner.

He smiled to himself. Vuk's thick new beard and dyed blond hair had transformed him so much that the name change seemed a necessary complement anyway. He looked like a Viking. Why not? Vikings went in for blood letting, pillaging and raping.

Josef came into the room with a towel wrapped around his massive frame.

"We're getting there, Thomas, we're getting there. Bergé's a cool guy, he's found me the perfect villa and he's introduced me to a bank director. He hasn't confirmed yet but the guy seems pretty flexible. I'm certain he just needs to be paid off. If it works, we're in clover. Money in the bank, credit cards, chequebooks, you name it. I'm getting nervous with that suitcase stuffed with cash lying in the hotel safe."

Josef paused as he drank a glass of fresh orange juice. Wash the taste of all those whores out of his mouth, he thought.

"That's one breed I don't trust, fucking bankers. Smooth, intelligent, hypocritical bastards. Highly paid professional bullshitters, worse than lawyers. Take you for every penny, given the chance. Anyway, if he does the laundering, you and I are going to become legal, Thomas. We're going to settle in this country and we're going to live like fucking Onassis."

Thomas nodded approval. He was going to get 500.000 US Dollars for himself. And Vuk would look after him. He'd look after Vuk too, until he got the money. Then he'd review the situation. He couldn't spend the rest of his life paying a moral debt to Vuk for saving him from those Bosnian Muslim pigs. He had his own ideas about running his life in the future, and they didn't necessarily include Josef or Vuk or whatever else he may choose to call himself.

Havel interrupted his thoughts: "O.K. Thomas, so what have you come up with? What's our little income generating pastime going to be? Cocaine? Heroin? How are we going to double our capital and have fun at the same time?"

Thomas looked at him and shook his head. "Neither, Vuk............"

Josef Havel didn't let Thomas finish his sentence:

"Josef, Josef, Josef," he roared. "Make that mistake again in public and you'll get us thrown into prison. Last warning Thomas." Havel looked very ugly for a few seconds.

"Sorry, sorry, cool it, it's because we're on our own." Thomas controlled his inner anger. He would get this bastard one day. Bring him down to earth. "Anyway, neither cocaine nor heroin. I've made a few enquiries. It's rougher out there than you would expect...... Josef. We can cope, we're rougher of course but why risk a knife in the back?"

Havel calmed down. "I can understand that, so what have you got up your sleeve?"

"Women, Josef, we're talking women," replied Thomas. "Most of the whores are working independently. Nobody has really got the market sussed out, it's waiting to be opened up and run like a proper business. If it's put on a proper commercial footing there must be millions to make, just by getting a cut."

"What do the cops do about the whores? Just turn a blind eye?" Havel couldn't hide his interest.

"The cops don't seem to mind, in fact the girls you see in the street and in the bars are legal. French law doesn't allow for brothels or pimping but you can sell your arse in the street without any problem."

Havel scratched his beard. "So what do we do? How do we get our cut and then what about the pimps? There must be some of them out there."

"Easy Josef, we just need a bit of time and between us we can scare the shit out of the whores and the pimps. Remember the Bosnian Muslims? Walk in the direction we want you to walk or die. That's simple effective medicine. We get our cut or they get an emotional rendezvous with me."

Havel laughed, his good humour restored. He was going to enjoy this. What a brilliant idea.

"Hey Thomas. Sorry about that. You know, flying off the handle. This is great. And I think it's going to be so fucking easy, like falling off a log. Let's go down to the bar and find our first recruits!"

# JEROME

KEEN INTELLIGENCE, a good sense of humour and unlimited energy made Jérôme the ideal assistant manager. He had worked his way up through classical banking channels and met Lucas at a time when the latter was in need of extra staff.

Lucas' natural charm and business acumen had led to faster than expected growth in his bank's local French clientele. But he was bored by the increasing administrative load and placed an advertisement for an assistant in "Les Echos". Jérôme was the first person to apply for the job and the two men took an instant liking to each other. He had now been with Lucas for seven years.

Jérôme was 35 years old, a computer and internet specialist. His only weakness was gambling in general and the Montecarlo casino in particular which he compared to Lucas' drinking: "just under control". He was married with three children and devoted his spare time to martial arts, ancient history and archaeology. The latter had led him, with his patient but less passionate wife, to Egypt, Syria, Jordan, Israel and Tunisia.

He was working on a theory about how the Mediterranean "cradle of civilisation" had fallen into decadence and stagnation, and the northern philistines (of whom he used to say Lucas was an eminent example) had taken over. The Celts, the Saxons, the Huns, the Picts and the Scots had shed their bearskins, skipped the tiresome business of taking thousands of years to build a decent civilisation and got stuck into conquering the rest of the world and developing trade. In the meantime, the great Greek and Egyptian civilisations had run aground somewhere B.C.

"You see," he tried to explain to a cynical Lucas, "nothing lasts forever, and when its gone it doesn't come back. I'm not just talking about death here, I'm talking about everything. Even the fucking planet is not going to last forever, is it? Let alone the stock exchanges you love following. When it's gone, it's gone.

"Like the Roman Empire: 2,000 years on and you still don't trust a Fiat do you? Ferraris and even Alfas, they're just glorious remnants of a glorious past. Look at you Brits. You are all nostalgic about the empire and all you've got left is a bunch of fucking monkeys in that shithole of a rock called Gibraltar."

"What a load of crap," was Lucas' summary. "My dad always said that anyone born and bred south of Calais is by definition lazy and degenerate and that just about sums up my world view Jérôme, particularly since I met you. Can't imagine why I gave you the job, come to think of it. So all of what you just said should be retracted immediately. Unless you want to be fired of course, for insulting senior management."

"I apologize profusely and retract everything I said."

"That's my boy," said Lucas patting him on the shoulder.

"That said............"

Lucas groaned. "Go on then, get it over with before I go to sleep."

"Well," said Jérôme " What's next on the list? What about the western world in general? What about China, what about the Muslims? Do you think they're working actively for our benefit? No way. One of them is going to finish us off economically and the other is going to blow us up. And our people at the top are going to make it so easy for them with their arrogant complacency that it's all going to be over in two decades."

Lucas took a wise contemplative walk round his office.

"In two decades young man," he said, "I'm going to be sixty fucking three and that's a bloody good time to go. You can still get it up, you can still eat, drink and be merry, you can still travel and play tennis and all that shit but you have this shadow hanging over you: you're beginning to stress out about old age, incipient incontinency and swollen prostate glands, inadequate pension and death. So if you pop off before the shadow starts eating you up and making you morbid you're a lucky man."

*Putain, ces anglais*: you had to hand it to them, thought Jérôme. They were so irreverent. Lucas in particular. Always taking the piss, always making light of issues which others obsessed about, always informal, always ready with a new joke.

He wondered how he had survived the years of routine, rigid hierarchy, bureaucracy and general inertia in the French bank. He would never have commanded the same salary and he would never have been able to develop a source of private income as he had with Lucas. And Lucas was straight with him, fifty-fifty on every deal, no argy-bargy.

His office looked out to the banking hall. On this particular morning he saw, as usual, Lucas entering, jaunty as ever, a kiss on both cheeks for Danièle, the receptionist, a handshake and a quick word with the cashier, another kiss for his secretary Solange and his usual greeting for Jérôme :

"Morning, creep. Fancy you being in at this hour." A wink, a sly look. Lucas walked into Jérôme's office.

" Good morning *Patron*," Jérôme replied. " I have a little something for you." Jérôme's use of the word *"Patron"* was an accepted irony. He sometimes accompanied it with an obsequious little bow.

"You've no idea how much I appreciate you, Jérôme, when you start the day with a *little something.* What is it?"

"The villa we put Eric onto. He's sold it. Half of his 5% makes..."

"Makes 2.5%," interrupted Lucas, "which makes 50,000 francs which makes 25,000 francs for each of us." Lucas rubbed his hands together and then pulled open his jacket with exaggerated gusto to indicate his inside breast pocket, staring at the ceiling as if offering a prayer of gratitude to some celestial provider.

Jérôme smiled. "Shit, you're really on form this morning boss. A walking calculator, that's what you are." He slipped a brown envelope over his desk which Lucas put straight into his pocket.

"That'll help us through to pay-day, eh, Jérôme? What was it that old comedian Coluche used to say? It's only at the end of the month that money starts running out, particularly during the last 30 days."

They laughed and walked through to Lucas' office. Jérôme sat down in his usual armchair and Lucas remained standing. The excitement and tension was building up inside him. He had to talk to his colleague and friend about Havel and work things out, size up the risks, establish a commission. Jérôme was his alter-ego, they bounced ideas off each other. They always found an answer in the end.

"Patron," Jérome would say, repeating the same worn out formula for the thousandth time, "if you go to bed with a stiff problem you always wake up with a solution in hand."

*"Okay, mon jeune ami.* I haven't told you about this new business opportunity because it's so potentially lucrative that I was worried your Latin excitability might just loosen your bowels before you could leave my office."

"Very considerate of you, patron," replied Jérome, wincing slightly at the gratuitous vulgarity.

"Listen," Lucas said, starting to walk round the office stroking his chin. "Eric introduced me to this guy, Czech nationality, with one fucking great suitcase filled with cash. Clean cash, well, you know, tax evasion cash which you and I approve of, not drugs or arms."

Jérôme raised his hand and Lucas stopped. "Sorry to be naive, boss, but how do you know?"

Lucas frowned. "Give me a break. I know the difference between Mafiosi and straightforward tax dodgers. I've met the bloke. He's like you and me, he drinks beer, plays tennis, chases women. He's therefore by definition OK. He sold a car distributorship and got paid 50% in cash. The rest is in Switzerland. Anyway, you know Eric's never introduced us to a crook".

"As far as we know, patron."

"Well we don't fucking well want to know, do we? How can you be sure about anything in life? How do you know your wife's not having it off with the plumber? Intuition. That's all. Things feel OK or they don't. Anyway, we're talking . . . wait for it, Jérôme, we're talking sixteen million dollars!"

Jérôme widened his eyes. *"Putain!"*

The most they had ever laundered in one go was three million francs – not even six hundred thousand dollars. They took 5% from the owner of the cash and 5% from the purchaser, if there was one. That meant three hundred thousand francs on their biggest deal. More often than not there wasn't a cash purchaser. The money was just channelled into a bank account in Liechtenstein and then transferred on.

A purchaser, or counter-party, was involved when they found someone who physically needed the cash.

The vendor's offshore bank account would be credited with a transfer from the purchaser's offshore account and the latter would keep the cash for local expenses – clothes, restaurants, trips to the casino, mistresses, boat maintenance, paying the maid, you name it. The vendor had probably accumulated the cash from undeclared cash payments entering his business, or from under-the-table cash from a real estate sale.

Lucas read Jérôme's thoughts. "Yeah, I know, it's a biggy. Big risks, big rewards, Jérôme. And anyway, is it intrinsically more risky laundering sixteen million than a hundred thousand?"

"Yes it is Lucas, and you know it. That kind of money makes an impact in the banking system. It gets noticed." Jérôme got up from his chair and started pacing up and down Lucas' office

"OK," said Lucas. "Let's treat it on a hypothetical basis. Let's say we agree to do it, agree the commission and Havel dumps the suitcase right here in the bank. First step?"

"Put it in the fucking vault and start praying to Allah."

They chuckled and unwound a bit. It took the tension out of the operation to remind themselves that they had the choice to refuse it. They unwound even further as they discussed the potential financial gain.

"Let's say we get 5%," said Lucas. "Eight hundred thousand dollars. That's four hundred thousand dollars each. *Ca mettrait du beurre dans les épinards, eh, Jérôme?* Jesus, it would keep me going, I can tell you. Even I would be able to save something out of that."

"Are you sure, Lucas? You wouldn't go and splash out on a fresh set of mistresses and blow the rest on booze?"

Jérôme, basically a sensible family man, had always been horrified by Lucas' spending habits.

" Yes of course, both, but I'd probably avoid the roulette table."

"*Touché* Patron."

%

Legislation covering money laundering was strong and strict and bold in intention but, back in the nineties, open to abuse in practice. It reposed essentially on the co-operation of the financial institutions, largely banks and insurance companies. The spirit of the law was that these institutions should report any transaction, notably cash, which "aroused reasonable suspicion". But then bankers and financial intermediaries were all greedy for new business, so there was a tendency, when lucrative new accounts were opened, to inverse the code and look for ways in which it would be possible to <u>not</u> be reasonably suspicious.

The accent, amongst many but not all, was on building an internal file which could be pulled out for the benefit of an internal inspector or external auditor – or in extreme cases the relevant government authority – and illustrate the diligence and thoroughness of the bank in vetting its customers before opening the account. Money laundering legislation, like most legislation, was a nuisance which had to be overtly respected and covertly ignored.

Money laundering was just disguising the origin of criminal cash and transferring it into apparently legitimate investments. Jérôme and Lucas had been deeply amused by and even admiring of a certain Vincento Piazza. In the early 1990's an Italian court confiscated assets worth one trillion Lire (590 million U.S. Dollars) from the poor man. They included 131 apartments, 122 warehouses, 20 factories, 10 school buildings and 250.000 shares in a Sicilian bank. Not bad for a builder with a declared income of 1.9 million Lire.

"He must have had lousy accountants," commented Jérôme. "I'd sue them for professional incompetence and incorrect advice. Pity he didn't know about Banque Helvas in Nice."

Lucas and Jérôme considered the legislation a nuisance indeed but easily circumvented, and they had never knowingly done any more than help clients avoid tax. Drugs and arms were strictly off limits for them. They were sincere about this.

But tax . . . frankly, what a load of hypocritical crap, was Lucas' view. Double standards, that was all. On the one hand, the most venerable banking institutions in the world had "Private Banking" operations in Jersey, Guernsey, Luxembourg, Switzerland, the Bahamas, Panama, Gibraltar, etc, and on the other, in their home territory or other foreign onshore countries, they vociferously preached the utmost care and caution vis-à-vis illegal money of whatever nature, including that originating from tax evasion.

So it was okay for Mr Dupont from France to deliver cash or arrange for a transfer to his secret and anonymous account in Luxembourg, but any fiscally illegal transaction onshore was expected to be reported. As Lucas said, if he advised Mr Dupont in Nice on how to set up a trust or an offshore company and park his assets in them, he could be incriminated by the *"Brigade Financière"*, be fined and jailed and lose his job. If he took Mr Dupont to Geneva and gave him the same advice, wearing his Banque Helvas Switzerland hat and succeeded in obtaining profitable business for the bank, he would be given a bonus.

"So what's it all about, Alfie?" Jérôme loved this weird expression, something to do with a 60's film apparently, and employed it frequently himself, provoking great mirth with Lucas because of his accent – *"So wotzeet ol aboat, Alphee?"*

Both men considered that drugs were at the root of the money laundering problem, not tax evasion, and both believed that the only solution was decriminalising the drugs in question, notably heroin. The drugs industry was estimated to have a 400 billion dollar a year turnover, making the likes of most FORTUNE 500 companies look pretty feeble. If cocaine and heroin were legalised and dispensed openly, the Colombian and Thai barons would lose their "raison d'être" and their cash would no longer be sloshing around the financial system. Or at least the trillions of existing dollars would not be increased.

But, for every haven that tried to crack down on laundering – and even a few diplomatic noises to this effect would result in money leaving and the haven losing income - there were a dozen others gleefully waiting to scoop up the fleeing loot. Lucas always said it was like global warming: everybody had to join in the fight. Otherwise, the chemical plants would just be dismantled in one country and set up in another.

They had gone through these considerations many times. In practical terms it just meant they had to be careful, but it never occurred to them that small "laundering" activities were immoral. They were just another service to existing and potential clients. And they found, as time went by, that very few of these clients were averse to participating.

Lucas maintained that there was even a macabre conspiracy behind much of the window dressing some banks indulged in but he was never precise, mumbling about Swiss entities (excluding his beloved Banque Helvas) sitting on ill gotten gains from the Nazi era, using them to finance their expansion abroad.

He quoted the scandal arising from the abortive attempt of one of the Swiss banks to shred documents relating to Swiss-Nazi financial arrangements which had led to a year-long series of revelations, conferences, threatened sanctions, international recriminations and a number of books, including *Nazi Gold* by Tom Bower and *Hitler's Secret Partners* by Isabel Vincent.

Lucas explained how according to these books the scandal had focused primarily on the personal tragedies of the "double victims", those who survived the Holocaust and then were denied their life savings by Swiss banks. Thousands of persecuted Jewish families entrusted their fortunes to the anonymity of a Swiss numbered account. While these same banks funnelled millions to fugitive Nazis in South America, the Jewish victims were systematically denied information or access to family accounts. Thousands were told, cynically, that funds could not be released without a death certificate to prove the demise of parents or siblings killed in Hitler's extermination camps.

In the immediate aftermath of the war, over a quarter of a million Jewish survivors languished penniless in Displaced Persons Camps for months or even years. The government stonewalled specific requests regarding bank accounts and blocked all attempts to use the huge amount of "heirless assets" for refugee aid.

There was, maintained Lucas on the basis of his reading, a fundamental issue regarding the role of the Swiss government in contributing to the Nazi's success in the first place.

The magnitude of the figures involved (many billions of dollars) demonstrated that this transfer of wealth was not simply a matter of lucrative theft; it in fact provided an essential lifeline for the Nazi war effort. The movement of Nazi gold to and from Swiss banks was pivotal in providing the hard currency the Nazis needed to obtain strategic raw materials not available in occupied countries.

The German state had exhausted all foreign exchange and Central Bank bullion by 1941. This precipitated a crisis which it overcame by looting the treasuries of occupied countries, melting down the bullion, stamping it with the Reichsbank symbol and funnelling it to the Swiss. By November 1942, this smelting operation came to include large amounts of dental gold, jewelry, rings, etc. The gold was sent and returned to banks in the form of gold bars, mixing together personal gold with "monetary gold."

Switzerland was the only country that would accept the obviously looted gold. The Swiss National Bank, the country's central bank, acted as a clearing house by purchasing the gold in exchange for foreign currency. It charged 0.5 percent and sold the gold to other neutral European central banks at higher prices. According to reports, the Swiss National Bank in Bern knowingly took in $400 million ($3.9 billion in today's funds) in looted gold between 1939 and 1945 in outright violation of international law, which prohibits banks from fencing stolen goods. The commission alone netted the Swiss $20 million (about $200 million in today's currency).

German corporations that required a foreign front in order to conduct their business operations would routinely set up a Swiss subsidiary. One of hundreds of such entities was I.G. Farben, the world's biggest chemical manufacturer, which produced the poison gas for concentration camps as a "patriotic duty." It established a Swiss international company, I.G. Chemie, which was protected from sanctions.

The Swiss could be described as "economically integrated into the German state". This integration carried over to the political sphere as well. Shortly after the passage of the infamous Nuremberg laws in 1935--which began the policy of "Aryanization", including the erosion of Jewish citizenship and the legal plunder of Jewish assets, the Swiss petitioned the Germans to have all Jewish passports stamped prominently with the letter "J".

The Swiss authorities were already blocking Jewish emigration. As the persecution became extermination, the Swiss worked harder to seal their borders.The number of Jews who successfully escaped to Switzerland, only to be dispatched back across the border to the waiting Gestapo, was estimated at 30,000 or more. Meanwhile, Nazi officials freely crossed, depositing their loot on a regular basis.

The Swiss financial agreements became an indispensable prop of the Nazi regime. But why was this permitted, and then overlooked by the Allies? And why was nothing done in the 1940s to provide justice to the Holocaust survivors?

Lucas, having expounded the above for at least the third time to his patient assistant, stood somewhat theatrically in the middle of his office. "Hypocrisy Jérôme, it's at the heart of the whole system, financial and political. Money makes the world go around..." (Please don't start singing that thought Jérôme)... "and if difficult issues such as millions of Jews being murdered and robbed get in the way then look the other way when cash is at stake. The same goes for drug money: pretend to get upset about it, spout sanctimonious bullshit and bank it offshore."

Jerome scratched his head and sighed resignedly. "Lucas, is this really the time to start going into all of that stuff? I know your opinions, you may be right, who knows? You're just quoting what you have read, do you believe unconditionally everything you read? Sometimes I get the impression you get all moralistic about things like this just to deflect your own mind from your personal issues!

" Come on now, how about the deal? Let's talk business."

"OK," replied Lucas. "You're right. Let's be positive about this."

*"Oui mon ami*, let's be positive and let's be realistic, 16 million dollars is enormous, we've never done anything remotely ressembling this. I mean we're talking a lot of shit if anything goes wrong, including a long spell in prison," ruminated Jérôme. "I suppose we can use the normal channels, but I'll have to speak to Fritz about

it. He may not like it. What's the time limit?" *Fritz* was Lucas and Jérome's nickname for Hans Teuber, manager of Baransteitbank in Liechtenstein.

"Well, I don't really know," said Lucas. "We only touched on the principle at the tennis club. My impression is he's got the cash somewhere, more or less safe, but he wants to get the ball rolling. His first priority is getting it out of France (he knows we can't do it in France) and at least put it into a safe. A bank safe. Then, in terms of banking it, I suppose he knows it will take time."

Jérôme scratched his head as Lucas watched his bright eyes and the slightly furrowed brow indicating concentration.

"Look, let's treat this on the basis of two separate steps. First step – apart from praying to Allah, that is – is get the fucking money into a safe. So we hire a safe at Baransteitbank and take the cash over in, say, ten different trips."

"Yeah, but we can't hire the safe in our own names, and Havel isn't going to want to do it in his name. Offshore company?"

*"Tu me surprends par ton intelligence, Patron.* I'll phone the lawyers in Gibraltar, get the company set up with nominee directors and shareholders and all the usual bullshit and then persuade Fritz to open an account in the name of the company. He'll probably insist on knowing who the beneficial owner is, i.e. Havel, but that's not a problem. We'll provide a character reference from Banque Helvas Nice. We'll rent the safe at the same time and Fritz will give me the key. Then we just cart the stuff over, one million or so at a time. When it's in the safety deposit box, step one is over and done with."

"And step two?"

Jérôme pondered the question. "Well, I don't know yet. Whatever happens, we can get the actual account open with a small initial cash deposit of, say, two hundred thousand dollars. Fritz won't object to that. Then we'll have to see."

"Hang on Jérome, Liechtenstein is one fuck of a way to transport cash, we'll have two or three frontiers to cross, we're just going to be multiplying the risks. Can't we do it in Monaco for God's sake, it's just round the corner?"

"*Patron*, how many times have I told you that you can't use Monaco for money laundering...........?"

"Please Jérome, please, don't use that expression, I hate it. We are not money launderers, we are financial and fiscal advisors helping someone to alleviate his tax liabilities. Anyway, what's so difficult about Monaco? It's got banks on every corner and where there's a bank there must be someone ..........."

"Someone supple and creative and intelligent like us, prepared to bend the rules?" interrupted Jérome. "Frankly I have no idea but there are too many controls there, the banks are monitored by this anti-money laundering outfit called SICFIN which is tough as hell and the reporting requirements would make it impossible to wash $16 million. The bank would be chewed to pieces, the manager thrown into prison and we'd be up shit creek with one very pissed off penniless client."

The relationship between Monaco and the French state in general (and Bank of France in particular) was sensitive. Monaco marketed itself to the international community as a tax haven, which indeed it was, but with the accent on attracting wealthy persons who, once officially resident and installed had zero income, wealth and inheritance tax (for direct family heirs) to pay.

But its relationship with France was different: same currency, overall financial regulation by the Bank of France, a resident French minister, etc. Last and not least, Monaco depended on electricity and water supplies from France. So it had to respect

France's insistence that French nationals could not become residents of Monaco and benefit from a "round the corner" tax break. And French residents, whatever their nationality, were by inference in the same situation.

"Who's going to have the signature on the account, Jérôme? Havel's told me he doesn't want any immediate connection between him and the cash."

"I'll find a solution", said Jérôme. "There's always a solution. We'll find a bona-fide Liechtenstein citizen and give him a power of attorney on the account. He can meet the courrier in Vaduz, deposit the cash in the safe and make gradual transfers to the account. Or maybe just give the power of attorney to the nominee directors in Gibraltar. They'll be able to give instructions to transfer the money or pay cash to nominated beneficiaries."

"Hmmm. Sounds good, *mon ami*. Excuse me asking, but who's going to do the carting of the cash? I can't do it – a lot of people know me over there and we can't use our usual little courrier, not for million dollar trips."

Jérôme looked at Lucas for a few seconds. He was obviously weighing something up in his mind. He looked calm and determined.

"I might just do it myself."

# DESTINY

NICE WAS A SMALL PLACE REALLY. When you cut out the residential areas and suburbs, the centre was barely more than a couple of square kilometres. And when its citizens went out there were no more than a dozen good restaurants to choose from. These included such names as "La Petite Maison", "Le comptoir", "Le Negresco", "Les Epicuréens", "L'Allegro", "Le Bistroquet" and "La Chaumière" on the hills above the town. A few notches down on the gastronomic league table were the bistro-style establishments such as "Le Félix" on Avenue Félix Faure, and "Flo's". There was also "La Barque Bleue" on the port, and of course "Le Yacht".

That so many people's personal destinies should start converging in Nice was a coincidence, or perhaps just an additional layer of destiny. But that they should physically crisscross each other was, if not inevitable, at the very least probable.

When Havel walked into "Le Yacht" on Wednesday evening he was exuberant and clearly limbering up for a good evening. On his arm was a sultry Mediterranean girl half his age, his pocket was stuffed with money and he had already drunk a bottle of champagne. The girl was obviously a pro, he'd met her in the Negresco hotel bar the same evening. Instead of taking her straight back to bed he'd decided to have dinner first.

George was behind the bar as usual and immediately remembered him from Bohringer's yacht. Havel had seen but not recognised him. The waiter looking after Havel's table took the order for champagne and passed it on to George, in the way all waiters in France passed orders to the bar, an authoritative loud statement: *"Une bouteille de Moët pour la 23. Deux verres, un seau de glaçons."*

George reflected on the situation. Havel obviously wouldn't make the connection and he didn't particularly want to start waving or introducing himself. It might look pretentious vis-à-vis the other waiters, it might be indiscreet vis-à-vis Lucas. He got the champagne out of the fridge, filled a silver bucket with water and ice and, having placed the champagne inside and draped a white napkin over the neck of the bottle, lifted everything onto the bar.

The waiter reappeared and took the bucket over to Havel, opened it with panache and poured out two glasses. Havel said something in the girl's ear, roared with laughter and swallowed the glass of champagne in one go.

The evening dragged on, for George anyway. The work was beginning to wear him down, he still had a deep fatigue somewhere in his recently broken bones and he was looking forward to getting home, back to Lucas' flat, comfort and the familiarity of being with his brother.

At 11.30pm Faruk slid open the hatch connecting the bar to the kitchen and pushed a large tray of washed glasses across for George to collect and stack. His hands stayed on the tray. His mouth locked half open and his eyes became motionless and black. He didn't move. George looked at him and tried to take the tray.

"Hey, Faruk, you okay? What's up? Let go of the fucking tray man."

Faruk slowly released his grip on the tray but still didn't move. He looked transfixed, hypnotised. He didn't say a word. George received a series of orders from the waiters for coffees and *digestifs* and reluctantly turned away to his work.

When he looked back three minutes later, Faruk was no longer there. Grabbing a momentary pause, he ducked under the opening on the right of the bar and hurried into the kitchen. The two chefs were smoking cigarettes, leaning back against the cooling ovens, looking white and unhealthy.

"Where's Faruk?"

*"Aucune idée, mon vieux.* He just dropped everything, took his jacket and left. Never seen him do that. Left the bloody taps running and pissed off. Something bugging him, probably some bird."

The two chefs exchanged world-weary glances and continued smoking. George went back to the bar. He noticed that Havel had left.

%

Faruk waited opposite the restaurant. He had his crash helmet on and sat astride his Kawasaki with the engine ticking over. The helmet's visor was partially lifted, just above his mouth, permitting him to smoke. His heart was thumping and his hands trembling. He was certain. The thick beard was new, the hair longer and a much lighter colour, but the set of the shoulders and the voice were virtually unmistakable.

He was not alone in knowing of Vuk Racik, nor was he alone in having physically seen him in Bosnia. He was however one of the few Bosnians caught in the centre of the conflict with Serbia to have both seen him and escaped massacre or starvation in the concentration camps. He thought back, allowing the pictures he had for so long tried to blur and forget, to resurface into his consciousness.

He and his sister Amra had spent the weekend with their university friends on the southern side of Craljna, a village some 20km outside Sarajevo. A small convoy of jeeps and trucks had driven directly past towards the centre. Within a few minutes they heard gunfire and panicked. Their whole family lived in the centre.

They drove their car as close as they dared towards their home, jumped out and ran desperately through the side streets leading to the back entrance of their house. Amra let herself in quietly and Faruk skirted round the side. The window he had hoped to climb through was locked so he returned to the back door which had been left open.

Amra was on her knees, mouthing silent screams, her arms around her naked, mutilated sister who was sprawled in front of their parents. The latter had their throats cut and lay in a circle of blood amidst overturned furniture and broken dishes. Their dog, Vishnu, a large black mongrel, was hanging from the flex of the ceiling light.

Amra was paralysed. Faruk retained just enough of his senses to register voices emanating from the sitting room, arguing over which pieces of furniture to loot. He vomited and staggered over to Amra. She had a dead man's vice-like grip on her sister and was breathing in tiny, rapid pants. He unfolded her tight embrace and lifted her still crouched body into his arms. He didn't feel her weight. His terror and revulsion blanked out his mind and gave him an electric strength as he carried her through the neat garden, passing the washing line. He saw the sheets and underclothes neatly pegged, stirring gently in the breeze. Through the fencing he could see the gap between their house and that of their neighbours.

Amra could see also. A tall, massively built man was smoking and giving orders to a dozen soldiers wearing Serbian paramilitary battle fatigues.

Josef Havel walked out of the restaurant at midnight. His good humour had been further enhanced by the meal and the way the girl had got his prick out under the table and made obscene but discreet signs to him with her mouth and tongue. He'd just managed to calm down his erection before leaving the table. A Mercedes pulled up and he was soon locked in a warm embrace.

The street lamps cast dappled light over Thomas' face as he drove his passengers in the direction of Antibes to where Havel had decided to move while waiting for the villa which Bergé had found him to be vacated. His eyes flicked occasionally up to the rear view mirror. He'd noticed Faruk while he'd been waiting outside "Le Yacht". The single beam of light from behind was confirmation that something was wrong. He'd already noted down the Kawasaki's licence number.

Thomas swerved right through a red traffic light, causing Vuk to swear. Faruk remained jammed between two cars. He'd lost them.

%

"So how do you work, you sublime creature?" Josef looked at his lovely companion in the back of the Mercedes and noted with approval the hardness in her eyes. He'd make her cry before the night was over. He'd break her into his rough habits and show her who was in charge.

"Work?" She rubbed her tongue sideways, from right to left, along her lower lip.

Josef smiled and then slapped her stingingly on the face. " Do you work for a pimp or do you work for yourself?"

The hardness stayed in her eyes , reinforced with a look of fury and despite the force of the blow she didn't cringe. She spat in his face and clawed the side of his cheek with the ferocity of a wild cat.

Josef gave her a second slap and placed his massive hand around her throat. He waited for the hardness in her eyes to melt and be replaced by panic, then despair. Then he released his grip and asked her the question again: "Pimp or independent?"

The girl started whimpering and appeared unable to talk. She gasped for breath and rocked forward. She was tougher than Josef imagined. He looked at the back of her head with a flicker of admiration. The car pulled up at a traffic light.

"I need a Kleenex," she moaned. Josef smiled and sat back as he lit a cigarette. The girl groped in her bag for a few seconds and then pulled out a metal canister, aimed it straight at Josef's face and sprayed him copiously with a powerful jet of gas. Josef was immediately stamping on the floor and screaming with fury and the pain of his temporary blindness. Thomas swivelled round to be met by another stream of gas which entered his eyes and nostrils.

The girl jumped out of the car and before she slammed the door shouted a threat which both men had used themselves on many an occasion: "Filthy Swine, mother fuckers, just wait. By tomorrow you'll both have had your balls cut off."

# WHAT TO DO

WHEN FARUK PARKED his motorbike outside the building where his studio was located, it was 1.00am. He was seething with rage and frustration. He'd driven back in a trance from the spot where Thomas had lost him, the ten minute journey a total blank in his mind. He kept reassuring himself: he'd lost them but he'd find them again. He'd lost them but he'd find them. Oh shit! He hadn't noted the car's licence number. But Nice was small. The Côte d'Azur was small. Prostitutes. That was it, prostitutes. He'd track him down. Racik was known to be an insatiable consumer of women, his reputation in Yugoslavia as a ruthless and obsessed Don Juan matching the one he had as a diabolically cruel and wanton murderer.

He walked slowly up five flights of stairs to his studio. The lift was buggered again. 1.10am. He had to speak to his sister. Amra would be asleep but it didn't matter. He hesitated and, before picking up the telephone, opened the window and dug his fingers into the rectangular pot he used for growing herbs. The soil fell onto the window ledge and he pulled out two plastic bags. He ran them under the tap and placed them on the table before opening them. The first one contained a revolver with five ammunition clips. The second contained a hand grenade. He looked at the weapons with the corners of his mouth turned down. His dark eyes blazed as he cleaned the gun.

All he had to drink in the studio was a bottle of Pastis. He carefully placed the bottle on the table next to the grenade, cleaned a glass and poured himself a large neat shot. He couldn't be bothered about the ice. Or the water. He lit a cigarette and sat tensely, staring at the telephone as he made up his mind about what to say.

"Amra?"

"Who is it? What's the time?"

"It's me, Faruk. I've got to speak to you."

"Faruk? Faruk? What's the matter? I'm still asleep. What's wrong?"

Faruk took a deep breath and calmed his voice, which was pitched too high. "That man. The one we saw. I've found him. He's here in Nice. He came to "Le Yacht" and I know it's him. Amra, I'm going to track him down and kill him."

There was a moment's silence as Amra rubbed her eyes and tried to understand. He could imagine her sitting up in bed, her lovely face, her bedroom in the flat she'd rented in the centre of Strasbourg.

"Faruk, what are you talking about? We agreed all of that was behind us now. What do you mean you've seen him? He's in Serbia, he must be. That's where he belongs, that's where he makes his living."

"Listen, I saw him. I wasn't sure at first but I am now. If you looked at the web-site I told you about you'd see he was born in Nice. God knows how or why but he started life right here. He's come back to his roots. Born in Nice and he's going to die in Nice."

Amra breathed deeply. Her mind was clearing, enough to know that her brother was embarking on a mad venture in the heat of the moment, which could get him killed. Faruk was all she had left in the world. They'd lived for two years together in Nice. The ache and loneliness of living as refugees with no family, anywhere, had made them stick to each other like glue. But Amra had realised, and had explained to Faruk, that their situation was becoming neurotic and unhealthy. They had to separate to build their own lives. She had found a job, thanks to her languages, within one of the E.U. sub-ministries located in Strasbourg and, tearfully, moved North.

"Faruk, don't do a thing until I get to Nice. Don't move, don't say anything, don't change anything. Go to work as usual. I'll be with you Saturday morning. I can't get there earlier. Promise?"

Angrily, Faruk promised. He returned the revolver and hand grenade to their cache, swallowed another two glasses of Pastis and spent a restless, sleepless night in bed with the light on.

The following evening, Thursday, he left work having said goodbye to George and drove to the old Nice, parking his motorbike directly in front of "Thor's", another of the town's pubs serving English beer and used as a rendez-vous for his friends. Saleh and Edouard were sitting upstairs listening to an amateur rock band, sipping Guinness and watching the groups of Swedish girls, mostly students and au-pairs, who congregated every night close to the band.

They were easy prey and each of Faruk and his friends had succeeded in seducing at least one in the past. Ahmed had even managed to fornicate in the pub's lavatories with a plump little blond called Emily. He'd never forgotten the experience. Nor did he fail to mention it whenever the loose, reputedly insatiable Scandinavian girls became a subject of conversation.

Faruk's cloudy demeanour put paid to his friends' high spirits. They ordered him a drink and asked what was wrong. Faruk was a brother, a brother in arms, and they would always listen, always help.

"Believe what I'm going to say because it's true. Vuk Racik is in Nice. I saw him in the restaurant, I followed him but lost him at some traffic lights." Faruk pursed his lips and waited for the reaction.

Stunned silence. Glasses held immobile between the table and their gaping mouths. Edouard slowly lowered his glass and stared first at Saleh, then at Faruk, who spoke again.

"Yeah, you heard me, Vuk Racik. Time to start thinking. Never mind how he got here. You know he was born in Nice so maybe he came back for old times' sake. He speaks French, so why not? It's his first big mistake and he's going to pay for it. Either we work out a plan between ourselves to kill him or I'll do it myself. I mean it."

"Hang on, hang on," said Saleh. "Cool it. Wait a minute. This is crazy. We were talking about him a couple of weeks ago. He can't be here. It's impossible."

They finished their drinks and walked out of the din and smoke into the Cours Saleya. Faruk's conviction was clear and unchallengeable; one way or another, with or without them, he was going to go ahead. Edouard and Saleh – and Ahmed who had been called on his mobile to join them – were unconditional friends but they didn't have the same personal reasons for killing Racik. Faruk's blind, intense hatred would make him take risks they would never take themselves. They reasoned with him, explained that a plan could only be established outside the heat of the moment.

Faruk agreed to wait for their next meeting on Saturday, after he'd talked to Amra, acknowledging reluctantly that trying to assassinate Vuk Racik on his own was absurdly dangerous and likely to fail. It was Saleh who managed to calm him down.

"If you try to do it on your own, the chances are you're the one who's going to get killed. Maybe that doesn't worry you. But what may worry you is this: Racik will know he's been located and he'll disappear to the other side of the world in a split second. Then we really will have lost him."

# CA SE COMPLIQUE

LUCAS AND JÉRÔME were waiting in the bank. Both felt the hiatus, sensed the turning point. They resembled each other despite their different lifestyles. Jérôme called it the Judeo-Christian factor. Deep down they knew, without formulating the words, that they had embarked on something which represented a new dimension. Both felt uneasy, both knew that they were stepping over their normal comfortable boundaries.

Lucas was right: bigger risks, bigger rewards. But there was a subconscious layer of remorse. Already, Lucas' bravado about knowing the difference between good and bad, between tax-evaders and criminals, was slowly evaporating. Deals of this size came once in a lifetime and . . . the flesh was weak.

They had already decided, as a sop to their moral misgivings, to say "10% or forget it" to Havel. But they could have pitched it higher to make him look elsewhere. Instead, they'd pitched it at a level where the monetary reward justified the moral sacrifice. This had been done tacitly.

Money had no smell, no colour. Those greenbacks were going to end up circulating in the USA or some banana republic in the Caribbean. The same kids who had coughed up their lungs, anaesthetised their brain cells and paid for their shot would end up with the same tacky notes (if that was where they came from) in their hands. Or perhaps a housewife or, why not, a charity, the Red Cross. God knew. Money was a means of exchange. The soiled hundred dollar note had passed from hand to hand, with no respect for the transaction. Money was morally exempt.

But the very fact that these similar rationalizing thoughts went through each man's mind indicated a process of justification. Perhaps every person and every thing carried a price. Lucas thought of retirement, just beyond the horizon. What if he went beyond the horizon and found himself penniless? Somebody else would have done the deal. And that somebody else would be sitting back on his veranda overlooking the sea with a cool drink and a beautiful companion so, if he didn't do it, it would be done anyway. So do it. If 'twere done, 'twere well 'twere done quickly.

It was 11.30am. The calming shots of JB were not calming him at all. It annoyed him that Jérôme stayed so clean and free of all his different crutches. His tobacco, his alcohol, his coffee.

It annoyed Jérôme that his partner and boss should be so weak.

///

Havel arrived at 11.40h. A bead of sweat rolled down his left temple. He carried a large suitcase, the size of a trunk, the same one he'd packed in the garage in Avar. His usual forced but convincing joviality was absent. He looked tense and slightly red in the face.

Lucas' secretary ushered him into the office and both Lucas and Jérôme rose to greet him.

"Josef, hi. You made it, well done. Let me introduce you to Jérôme. He's my alter-ego. If you ever need to talk to me and I'm out, ask for him."

Havel's frame of mind was reflected in his laconic response. "OK. Now tell me what we're going to do with this." He lifted the suitcase onto Lucas' desk. Lucas winced. One scratch on that beautiful mahogany would ruin it.

Despite his churning stomach, Lucas, a master of self-control, radiated calm and the right degree of seriousness. It was the best way to deal with certain clients who had always got what they wanted, the ones who tended to bulldoze.

"There are a number of steps involved, Josef. Sit down first and let me get you a drink." He poured Havel a glass of his Glenmorangie and another shot of J.B. for himself.

"Jérôme, do you feel like something?" He knew the answer of course, but these sort of social gestures alleviated the tension. Jérôme shook his head.

"Okay, Josef. We'll go into detail later on but this is it in a nutshell. We will first of all count the money in front of you and then put it into the vault. Safety first, you'll agree. We will then form an offshore company for you with nominee shareholders and directors and open an account in Liechtenstein. The statutes of the company will indicate that its main object is the negotiation of refined oil contracts with the Middle East and subsequent supply thereof to luxury yachts in the Mediterranean.

"A letter of recommendation will be obtained from the lawyers forming the company which will also explain that the nature of the business and the clients involves cash payments. The funds will be transported in say twelve different trips and physically locked up in a safety deposit box rented by the company, and with one key holder: a Liechtenstein citizen, so it all looks normal."

Lucas spread his hands to indicate the logic was obvious. "We will negotiate with the bank manager, who will have to be paid of course, so that a blind eye is turned to the cash deposits on the account which will take place gradually, in fifty thousand to two hundred thousand amounts. The first deposit will take place the day we arrange the first trip. Transport of funds will be spread over two months and all the cash will have been flushed into the company account by November, i.e. within six months."

There was a moment's silence. Havel's head was spinning. All this stuff about offshore companies, bankers in Liechtenstein being paid off, nominee shareholders. Lucas' delivery had been smooth and businesslike but Havel didn't really understand.

He knew how to send a truckload of ammunition across the border, or even ship a tank over to Libya. And he knew how and when to pick up the payment and what precautions to take. But this was a different world. Good thing he'd spoken to Eric Bergé beforehand, or he might have walked into the first bank he'd found. Eric had told him he would be refused and possibly reported, or accepted and definitely reported to TRACFIN, the French money laundering control centre. And that would have been that.

"Sounds OK so far. All I need is your reassurance that not one cent of my money gets lost on the way. What guarantees do I have? And when can I start drawing on it?"

Lucas maintained his steady pose and looked Havel straight in the eyes. "There are no guarantees, Josef, except me and Jérôme. You either trust us or you don't. We can't even give you a receipt. Your security is what you feel about us. We can give you the share certificates relating to the company, we can give you the key to the safety deposit (although I strongly advise against this) when you want it, and we can give you statements on the company account showing the cash deposits. But it you want total anonymity, which is what you told me, we can't give you a signature. You'll have to wait until an account in your own name is opened with us, initially in Switzerland I suggest, which is when we start transferring from the company account directly to you. Then you'll have everything you want, including your residence permit. Jérôme will get that sorted out for you.

"You can transfer as much as you want of your capital from your personal account in Switzerland to your account in France without arousing any suspicion, you'll just be another foreigner making the wise decision to settle in the south of France!" Lucas stopped with this last observation which he thought a perfect preliminary conclusion.

Havel wiped the corner of his mouth with his huge paw, looking more than ever like a dangerous, sulky bear. Jérôme was watching him attentively.

"Why is this all so fucking complicated?"

Lucas allowed himself a polite laugh, meant to convey an impression of resignation and patience natural to a man who'd had to cope with the complexities of the financial system for so many years.

"You may well ask, Josef. The problem is the following. You know and we know that your money doesn't come from drugs or arms dealing. But the authorities don't. So if they sniff 16 million dollars – which is enormous by any standards – they will automatically assume the wrong thing. In fact, you would be judged guilty until you proved your innocence.

"And to prove your innocence, you'd have to explain where it really came from. And that would upset both the guys who bought your car dealership and the Czech tax authorities who would want to square up a few accounts with you. Whether or not," added Lucas for dramatic effect, "Czech tax authorities can get you chucked into prison like they can in France, I don't know. But you've got to do it our way I think. *Piano piano.* In fact, we may even form a second company and open an account in Switzerland to make the money even more difficult to trace."

The last question was hovering in the air. Lucas couldn't decide whether to state his price or wait until Havel asked him. Jérôme intervened.

"Excuse me, Lucas, I think it's important we inform Mr Havel of what all this is going to cost."

"You're right." Lucas cleared his throat. Another vaguely digested Shakespearean quotation floated through his mind. Something about tides in the affairs of man which, taken at their flood, led on to fortune . . . or you missed the fucking boat because you were wandering up and down the quay trying to make up your mind.

"This is a costly business with controlled risks, but risks all the same. Formation of companies, physical transport of millions of dollars across national borders, paying off the Liechtenstein bank manager, paying off the Gibraltar lawyer, paying the guy who will have the power of attorney to sign on behalf of the company until the shares are transferred on to you . . . This is a major operation, Josef, and it's going to cost you 10%. You may be able to find a cheaper deal elsewhere but you won't get the Rolls Royce treatment we're offering."

Havel smiled. He took one fifty thousand wad out of the suitcase and placed it on the desk to one side. He then closed the suitcase and narrowed his eyes.

"10% means 1.600.000 dollars, and that's too much. I was counting on 5%, i.e. 800.000 dollars. I'm not going to sit here and negotiate all morning. I settle for 1.000.000 dollars now or go to another bank. The fifty thousand sitting in front of you is a down payment. Take it."

Lucas and Jérôme remained silent, both feeling slightly embarrassed. They didn't know this man well enough and this was not what they had agreed between themselves. The silence deepened. They knew there was no point in arguing or whining about expenses. Havel knew his offer was adequate.

"We'll take it," said Lucas.

# THOMAS

%

THOMAS WAS A SIMPLE MAN. He wanted money to be able to disappear to a simple, warm place, Crete maybe, and live a simple life on his own. People bored him, left him completely indifferent. They simply didn't count, any more than any other species of life. He'd never had any relationship of any kind apart from with his father who was a paedophile and a drunkard and had sodomised him until the age of thirteen and forced him to labour on his farm from the age of five. When Thomas decided that he'd had enough, he had loaded the disgusting old man's shotgun and blown away his father's head when he was lying, unshaven and inebriated, in bed. The police had found the child sitting on the front steps leading up to the house, apparently shocked into dumbness by the appalling scene in the bedroom. The social services rallied and placed the boy in an orphanage. Thomas was sent, two years early, to do military service after he'd nearly strangled and gouged out the left eye of another inmate who had had the misfortune to try to put his hand on his buttocks.

Thomas excelled in all the military arts and met Vuk Racik in 1993. The latter had stormed into a cottage near Sarajevo where Thomas was tied to a chair and being questioned by two Bosnian Muslims wearing masks. The interrogators were briskly disposed of, Thomas liberated and the new duo had been formed.

The men worked as partners, protecting each other, and while Vuk wreaked his manic, savage mayhem on the Bosnian Muslims, Thomas mopped up potential danger behind his back. Vuk was wild and murderous until he got bored and wanted to change his lifestyle and move abroad with his earnings. Thomas was calm and ruthless but, if Vuk had taken the time to ponder his case, disturbing because he had no feelings, no moral structure. Vuk worked his bloody way across Yugoslavia in the name of Serbian supremacy and to avenge the suffering of the Serbian minorities in the Croatian, Bosnian and Kosovan republics. He had a cause.

Thomas had none, and no one would ever count apart from himself. Even Vuk's combination of intelligence and contempt for mankind could not quite register what Thomas really was: inhuman. Or dehumanised, if one was to be charitable. The result was the same, because Vuk would never have imagined that his protégé and guard might be a danger to him.

Thomas quickly gained an understanding of the market for prostitutes in the Nice area. He was subtle and set out first to find the girl who had made such a fool of him and Josef and second to garner information by being Mr. Nice Guy with a couple of whores every night.

He tried all the best bars including the Negresco but didn't see nor, after discreet enquiries, hear anything that could lead him to find his prey. He concluded that she had been so frightened that she had left Nice to ply her trade elsewhere, possibly Marseilles.

So he concentrated on his business plan and with his rapidly improving French soon discovered that his initial observations appeared correct: the market was open because there was no more than a loosely connected group of pimps operating with between seven and ten girls each. None of the big Parisian or Marseilles operators appeared to be present and about half of the girls were independent. He reckoned they could be gradually coerced into working for him and Josef but stealing girls from the pimps was going to be another matter.

He explained this to Josef who, slightly drunk, immediately gave his action plan:

" We'll make a proposal to one of the pimps and he'll refuse because we won't look dangerous enough. He'll go and tell his other little pimp colleagues about what happened, maybe even boast about how he scared us off. Then we approach another one. Same story. And a third one.

"That's three *refusniks* and the pimp community are beginning to wonder who the jokers are. We then make the three *refusniks* disappear (permanently of course) and let their girls know who is now in charge. The other pimps will be shitting in their pants because they have never seen what real war means and will come to us begging for mercy and a job."

Thomas kept a straight impassive face. "Nice and simple Josef. How are you intending to get rid of the three refusniks and how long before the surviving pimps or the girls report us to the police?"

Josef yawned and poured out some more champagne. "Getting rid of doesn't mean a public execution, Thomas. It means make disappear in a way which could never be traced to us although our pimp friends know it can't be anyone else and so they start shitting themselves, like I said. By the way Thomas, just how deep is the Baie des Anges?" He started laughing. "I'm not joking, how deep is it?"

Thomas didn't laugh. This was ridiculous. They weren't operating out of Serbia or Bosnia. They were nobody here. France was a structured society with a police force which was relatively uncorrupted and an independent judiciary. He recognized that he himself had been too simplistic in his original proposal to Josef.

"Josef, let me do some more research. We've got all the time in the world and we can get it right. I'm all for pre-emptive action but I have a feeling we need to go slowly here. When we get it properly structured we're looking at income for life. And we have a lot of fun too. No point in screwing it up by storming in without evaluating the real risks."

Josef nodded. "Yeah, I know. I wasn't really being serious. But someone's got to get scared somewhere along the line because even in the extreme case that we build up our own business from scratch we'll still be stealing indirectly from the pimps, poaching on their territory. They won't like that either so you see we'll have to get nasty anyway."

Thomas looked at Josef. Never underestimate him, he realised. The guy was no fool for all his brutality. He was obviously thinking even further ahead than himself.

"Build up our own business? You mean just take over the independent whores and leave the pimps to themselves?"

Josef lit a cigarette and narrowed his eyes. He smoked for a couple of minutes in silence.

"Ever thought of importing brand new merchandise Thomas?"

Thomas nodded his head slowly. Of course. They already had a chain of Eastern European girls which they had used to service the top government officials and civil servants back in Yugoslavia. They could re-establish contact.

"Fucking brilliant Josef."

"Thank you Thomas, not bad eh? Anyway, you continue the good work, prepare the ground, I'm going to make a few calls. Oh, and find me that bitch who blinded us the other night Thomas. I want to deal with her personally."

Thomas pursed his lips. "I'll take over where you leave off."

%

While Thomas kept himself busy with his new business venture he still found time to track down the owner of the motorbike. He'd informed Josef of the problem, who'd spoken to Eric Bergé, telling him that his Mercedes had been scratched and he wanted to locate the owner of the offending vehicle.

Bergé knew his way backwards around the police commissariats and town hall, and the same morning telephoned through Faruk's name and address. Thomas left Antibes with instructions to kill him, but not before finding out why he had followed them and who else might be involved. He drove to a spot just fifty metres from Faruk's block of flats, checked out the back of the building to see if there was access which could be made without his seeing anyone from the front and, satisfied, sat patiently in his car, smoking, until 1.00am.

Faruk's Kawasaki could be heard in the still of the night before the beam of light from its headlamp appeared. Thomas left his car and waited in the shadows until he saw Faruk put the key in the lock of the main entrance door. As he pushed it open, Thomas moved silently forward and stepped inside, a few feet behind.

Faruk looked over his shoulder and saw Thomas smiling at him with a silenced revolver in his hand. He stopped with his first foot on the stairs and stared.

"Faruk, Faruk. Let me introduce myself. Sorry to drop in so unexpectedly. My name is Thomas, and we have a few things to chat over."

"What are you talking about? Why are you pointing that thing at me?"

"Depending on the outcome of our chat I may not need to point it. Take me up to your flat, Faruk, or our conversation may end a little prematurely."

Faruk started climbing the stairs slowly. Nobody, but nobody, could be so interested in chatting to him that he needed a gun to persuade him, unless there was a connection with Racik. Shit and fuck. What an amateur he was, what a schoolboy. It wasn't he doing the tracking, it was them. They'd seen him that night on the motorbike. He began to sweat.

He opened the door and stood in the middle of his studio, watching as Thomas sat down, placed the revolver on the table and looked around. The man was obviously not afraid that Faruk might try to jump him. He was used to being in control.

"Sit down", he said. His words were quiet, polite but impossible to disobey. "OK, who do you think you were following the other night?"

"I don't know", said Faruk. This was it. He'd had it.

"Let me help you. You were following Vuk Racik. I was driving." Faruk remained silent. "I'd like to know why. You weren't planning on doing him any harm, were you? What is he to you, Faruk? Tell me now or you lose your first kneecap."

"Fuck you, you murderous bastard. You're one of his psychopathic henchmen, are you?"

Faruk got no further. Thomas reached across the table, grabbed his hair and pulled his head down viciously, smashing the bridge of his nose and his front teeth onto the formica surface.

"Cut the shit, you little Muslim runt. This is your last chance to stay alive. Why were you following Racik and how come you know him?" Thomas' eyes showed disdain. His back straightened.

"Vuk Racik and his hooligans killed my parents. They raped and tortured my sister to death. I recognised him at the restaurant and followed him when he left. I didn't know what I wanted to do after that." He wiped his face gingerly, hopelessly trying to stem the tears of terror and rage. He felt desperate and dominated to a degree he had never experienced. The hatred in his body was turning to liquid fear in his bowels. He had to keep some minimum of self-respect, of control.

"And do you know now? You want to kill him, don't you? Well, that just doesn't suit me right now, my friend. This is not the moment . . ........"

If Faruk had listened to the rest of what his adversary had to say, he would have grasped the significance of the words. Not right now . . . not the moment . . . but he gave himself only a few minutes to live and his brain was focused on dying. And how not to die.

At his feet, against the table leg, stood the half-finished bottle of Pastis. He scratched his knee, lowered his hand further and grasped the neck of the bottle. One chance, one movement. He brought it up behind his shoulder and flung it into Thomas' face. It smashed into jagged shards, Thomas fell backwards off his chair, blinded by the Pastis and screaming with shock and pain.

In two seconds, Faruk was out of the door and running down the stairs three at a time. In thirty five seconds he had reached his motorbike. He unchained it, started the motor and accelerated wildly, the front wheel lifting as he just managed to keep control. He saw Thomas running out of the building, clutching his face with one hand and raising his gun with the other.

Faruk made one mistake, a forced error. An articulated lorry in front of him and on-coming traffic made him slow, just in time to see the approaching exit for the motorway from the Ariane in the direction of Ventimiglia, Italy. With no time to think, he took the exit and accelerated again, through two red lights and onto the rising lead-in. The next exit was 10 kilometres away. He saw the rev-counter rising into the red and changed up to fourth. When he hit the last bend, he lost control.

Thomas arrived one minute later. He saw the Kawasaki lying on its side. Underneath it, impaled on the handle-bars, was Faruk's body. He had to be dead. He drove on, cursing. Stupid bastard, stupid fool, stupid fucking cretinous little shit. He would have to make other plans. This had been his best opportunity so far to get Vuk killed, by someone else, and steal his money.

%

There was a hushed silence among the motorists who had stopped as the ambulance arrived. Faruk's battered body was totally immobile and to the horror of all present the handlebar of his motorcycle appeared to have pierced his chest. Nobody had dared approach him, all could see he was dead; it was only the experienced ambulance men who could see that the body was still alive, just breathing and emitting a tiny pulse. They put him on a drip and placed an oxygen mask over his face as they waited for the police to bring the necessary equipment to saw off the handlebar. They gave him a few hours to live.

# A BREATHER

THE TWO BROTHERS sat comfortably together in Lucas' living room.

" . . . So he drives all the way from London to Glasgow, non-stop, and by the time he gets there he's fucking exhausted and fucking dehydrated . . ."

"Rather a lot of 'fucking' going on, isn't there?" commented George.

"That's none of your fucking business....." Resigned smile from George, wink from Lucas. "Anyway, the one thing he needs, more than anything else in the world, is a pint of beer. So he goes into this pub, which is crammed with what looks like the whole of the local Glaswegian community, and makes his way to the bar......."

When things got a bit silly, as they always did with Lucas, certainly when he was on form and life seemed one long hilarious joke, George began to let himself fuse with the idea that maybe life really was just that, maybe the only approach was to laugh at the absurdity of everything, particularly death which rendered all endeavours futile?

"......one funny thing he notices, nobody is fucking drinking. He doesn't give it a second thought and orders a pint of the best local bitter, swallows it in one go and the barman says 'That'll be tuppence, Sir.'" George raised his eyebrows to express interest. "'What tuppence?' says the bloke, 'You must be joking! That would cost me two quid in London.'"

"Come on, Lucas. Get it over with." He flicked the side of his glass with his fingernail, enjoying every minute of the mediocre story.

"Shut up. So the barman says 'Och aye' and explains that it's the local brewery's centenary and all the pubs have been asked to sell their beer, just for this evening, at the same price as it was sold a hundred years ago. Are you with me?"

"Just about, Lucas. I must admit the intrigue is getting a bit complicated, but go on." The drowsy contentment of the old ritual. That was another point: repetition, time-honoured traditions which gave continuity and duration.

"So the bloke says, 'Great, I'll have another one, but tell me, why is no one else drinking?' and, laughter as Lucas slaps his knee, "the barman replies that they're all waiting for Happy Hour."

It wasn't the jokes that George enjoyed so much as Lucas' performance. It made everything seem normal and happy. The day his brother stopped would mean something had gone seriously wrong. But for the moment he seemed even more exuberant than usual. But his exuberance was tinged with nervous energy of late, particularly this evening.

"Tell me, how's business, Lucas? Everything under control? How's the big deal?"

Lucas rose to pour fresh drinks and both men lit a cigarette. A half-finished pizza lay on the table in front of them, together with a game of backgammon. A video cassette was on the television, ready to be watched as soon as they had finished eating. They had decided to reserve one evening a week together and had developed an easy-going routine which both enjoyed and looked forward to.

"Yeah, well, it's warming up considerably to tell you the truth. I can't really go into details, it's all a bit technical, but things are underway. It's going to be a bit long and drawn out but worth it. Seriously worth it."

"And Havel? No further insights into who he is and what makes him tick? I saw him the other night in Le Yacht. He was with a nice bit of Italian pussy. Blimey, he knocks back the old booze, doesn't he? Mind you, given his size maybe that's normal. Bit of a brash bugger. Sorry to keep asking this but are you sure about him? I mean, are you sure it's safe to do business with him? I got the occasional funny vibe when I saw him, don't know what exactly, but just something . . ."

"Come on, George."

"Well . . . frankly, a bit lethal. I just wouldn't want to cross swords with him. Probably a load of bollocks like you told me last time."

Lucas weighed his words. Everything George had said reflected his own misgivings and feelings of apprehension. Havel basically scared him, but he didn't want to admit it either to his brother or to himself.

"He's a tough cooky but I don't think he'll try to screw me. In fact, he's already paid part of my commission up-front. The thing is I've basically got him by the balls. He's left his assets more or less completely under my control and he needs me. He needs me more than I need him."

"What kind of assets?"

George watched his brother attentively. He was squirming, no doubt about it. Cash. He was certain. It had to be cash or Lucas wouldn't be so evasive.

"I'd check out pretty carefully where he got his 'assets' from, Lucas. And whatever happens, I'd make sure I didn't lose any of them. Havel might take that badly, take it as a threat to his future consumption of whores and champagne."

Whores and champagne, *le cul et le fric*, thought Lucas. Damn George, he was talking to him a bit like their father used to, that cocktail of wisdom camouflaged by dry humour which always made him reluctantly be honest with himself. And to be honest, brutally honest, he was beginning to feel shaky about the whole deal. Have another drink.

He searched, unsuccessfully, for another joke to change the course of the conversation and the sudden change in mood.

# FIGHT

JOSEF HAVEL walked into the Martinez Hotel on the Croisette in Cannes and listened to some jazz. He cast a slightly jaundiced eye over the small stage, the bar and the other people drinking and chatting. Within a few minutes he found the atmosphere too tame for him and he sauntered out again and then down to the "Tonga", a nightclub with a superb selection of girls.

The girls started to dance, some on the tables, when the music heated up and the patrons, some regulars and some tourists, swallowed their inhibitions with their bottle of St. Emilion. Josef ordered a bottle of champagne as was his wont and settled down in a corner to decide which girl he would approach. He knew the rules of the game in the Tonga: no overt picking up and carting off for sex; stick around, drink, contribute to the general atmosphere and after 1.30h or 2.00h a.m. negotiate discreetly with whomever tickled your fancy.

He focussed on a blond woman who wore a long transparent skirt through which he could see the outline of a black G-string and matching bra. She gyrated beautifully to the music, pushing forward her lower abdomen in a shameless mime of fornication. Josef felt the usual immediate response between his legs and smiled at her, beckoning her to try his champagne.

She swooped, took his glass out of his hand and was away again, dancing and waving the glass above her head. She swooped back to his table and sat on his knee, panting and laughing.

Havel wanted to have some more fun before taking her back to his new found short-let apartment on the Cap d'Antibes and therefore didn't mind playing by the rules of the establishment and making his move after 1.30h a.m. He stayed until 2.00h a.m. The girl flounced from one man to another, teasing each. It was impossible to tell which one she would choose. But Havel knew.

She had asked him to wait outside when she gave the signal, a bit further up the Croisette. For some reason she didn't seem to want anyone to see her leave with him. When the time came he stepped outside as demanded and strolled slowly away to the left of the entrance to the club.

In the ladies' toilet, the girl pulled out her mobile phone and called Yves Delaunay.

"It's definitely the guy Madelaine told us about. Big, very big, blond hair and wearing a beard. He told me the same bullshit he told Madelaine, ordered the same champagne. He says he's on his own. I'll go with him only if I see you waiting outside. And by the way , you'd better bring Alain and Philippe. He's kind of scary."

Yves Delaunay made a small tight-lipped smile. He was ex-Foreign Legion, a strong and dirty fighter. He called both his thugs nevertheless. It only took a few minutes for them to arrive and climb into his car which he'd parked some thirty metres from the entrance to the club.

The girl emerged alone from the club, freshly coiffed and with renewed lipstick and makeup. She walked towards a now slightly impatient Josef. He took the back of her neck in his strong tanned hand and guided her, like a child, along the Croisette in the direction of his car.

The traffic had thinned by now and Cannes' nightlife was definitely drawing to a close. A group of four youths drove past with a surreal blast of techno music emanating from their car which seemed to shake the palm trees. They looked stoned and bored. On the other side of the road some American tourists staggered and swayed towards the Carlton, the sea beautifully calm on their left, reflecting the lights of the town and those of the yachts moored in the bay.

Yves Delaunay watched Josef and the girl walk back towards the Martinez and then up a small street on the left running towards the end of the Rue d'Antibes. Josef's car was parked opposite a church. The street was relatively dark and, Delaunay noted with satisfaction, totally emptied of people. He slipped the car into a small space and doused the lights.

He spoke to the two vicious looking thugs sitting in the car behind him without turning his head, his hands still on the steering wheel.

"He's a big bastard which means he's going to hit the ground very hard. I don't want any mistakes, no time for him to shout. Phil, you hit in the throat if you can and Alain, you make sure he goes down. We've got to get him lying down, then we kick the living shit out of him but we don't black him out. He's got to understand what's going on.

"I want him to be so terrified he never comes back to the Côte d'Azur. Same treatment for his little friend who Madelaine told us about. I'll ask him personally where we can find him."

Delaunay got out of the car and walked casually towards Josef with Philippe at his side. Alain followed on the other side of the street.

Josef had noticed them as soon as the car had pulled up at the Tonga. His personal alarm system, as he called it, was as sharp as that of a cobra. It was not that three men sitting in a car which had appeared a few minutes after his leaving the club meant anything *per se*. He just made a mental note that if he saw them again they spelled danger. If they got out of the car and came towards him it spelled emergency. And Josef handled emergencies well. He'd been handling them for years all over Yugoslavia and he'd learned to adapt to every permutation in the book.

Philippe and Alain didn't worry him. Delaunay was something else. He could tell by the set of his shoulders that the man was a soldier. His arms were swinging casually, he had that measured disciplined gait. Years on the parade ground. Tough bastard was Josef's conclusion.

He made a quick assessment of his options and decided to take out Alain first. Chatting and laughing he crossed the street with the girl, pretending he wanted to look more closely at the church.

"I'm sure a nice girl like you says her prayers before going to bed." He slid his hand up the back of her skirt and inside her panties. "You're going to say them again after going to bed tonight as well, you're going to be praying for more, more of Josef's cock."

The girl laughed nervously, tensing as Josef ran his hand across her buttocks. She felt very small and very frightened despite Delaunay's presence. The power and size of Josef was one thing but there was something else which terrified her. He was transmitting a message to her. The message was that he knew and that she would be punished for her duplicity. The last dregs of her drink fuelled courage and high spirits leaked out of her body.

"Hey, what's the time for God's sake?" Josef asked, as if suddenly aware that it was terribly late. He looked at his watch as if it had stopped, discreetly holding her left wrist with his right hand so she couldn't reply.

"Excuse me Mister, have you got the time?" He posed the question to Alain, who was now within a couple of metres, with such a neutral and polite tone that Alain automatically looked down at his watch. A split second later Josef punched him so hard in the middle of his face that his nose was pushed inside his skull. Alain died instantly, as if he'd been hit by a freight train.

Josef spun the girl round so she was between himself and Delaunay who was approaching from the right with Philippe. Neither had enough time to properly register what had happened before Josef spoke again, calm and polite.

But he felt the familiar fury seeping into his limbs.

"Can I help either of you gentlemen?" He took the girl's hair in his left hand and made a short jerk. She whimpered, her eyes closed.

Delaunay put out his hand to stop Philippe from closing in. Too late. Philippe was strong and confident and wanted to show Delaunay his mettle. He could handle Josef. He moved lithely round to Josef's left and launched a lethally powerful punch at the side of Josef's face. Delaunay faltered for a second and then moved in from Josef's right.

Josef pulled the girl's head round and back. Her neck snapped as she caught the full force of Philippe's blow on the temple. Josef threw the doll like corpse between himself and the three metres separating him from Delaunay.

The latter was momentarily shocked by the speed of events and above all by the limp body of the girl lying at his feet. He liked this girl, her vivacity, her decency. He slept with her occasionally and protected her from the various unsavoury predators she inevitably met when plying her trade. He stooped involuntarily, his arms spread. Josef took two lightning steps forward and kicked him in the front of the neck with a rugbyman's strength and precision. He side-stepped as he anticipated Philippe's cosh coming down on his head and received the blow on his left shoulder. The pain was considerable.

But he spoke calmly: "Oh dear, oh dear, are you going to pay for that you fat piece of shit."

Philippe looked scared by now. This was not going to plan. His friend Alain was still lying inert in the gutter and his boss was rolling around in the middle of the road, gurgling and clutching his throat, eyes bulging. He pulled a six inch knife from behind his back and concentrated, every muscle tensed.

Josef held off, gaining time, waiting for the numbness in his shoulder to dissipate and pulled his own knife from its leg sheath. How many Bosnian Muslims' throats had he cut with that? A couple of dozen at last count. This made him smile.

"You're not a Muslim are you by any chance? If you are, start praying to Allah my friend. If you're not it's not going to make a whole lot of difference."

Philippe circled him, crouched and dangerous as a cornered beast but diminished by his growing fear. He rushed his opponent, carrying his knife at shoulder level with his right arm, his left arm forward, fingers splayed. Josef's knife came round in an arc and ploughed into the man's stomach from left to right. The worst way to die.

"That's for my shoulder. Now I either leave you like that and it will take you about one hour to die or you tell me what all of this is about." He glanced back at Delaunay who was still totally incapacitated, gagging for breath, both hands at his throat.

Interesting, thought Josef, the man still had some dignity, reflected from his eyes which showed no fear nor hate, just a fatalistic acceptance that this was the end. Not many like that, even amongst his best men in Serbia.

Philippe saw a gleam of hope. Maybe if he told Josef what had motivated the attack he would be spared. Maybe this fearsome giant standing above him would call for an ambulance before leaving. Maybe he could explain it only came to knives because things got so unexpectedly out of hand.

"It's the girl. Madelaine."

Josef lowered his face closer. The bastard could barely whisper. "Who the fuck is Madelaine?"

"The girl you hit, the girl you were going to beat up in Nice. She asked us to find you and teach you a lesson. We weren't going to kill you, I swear it." He held his hands against his stomach to staunch the flow of blood. The pain was intolerable. Too much to scream, even to do more than whimper.

"Oh yeah, Madelaine, that was the stupid bitch's name was it? I never had more than a bit of slap and tickle with the dirty slut. So where is she now?"

Philippe could only just mouth the words. "Here. In Cannes."

"Thanks pal."

Josef heaved Delaunay over beside Philippe. "It's been fun getting to know you both."

He stared both men in the eyes for a few seconds and gave them a facetious little smile as he drew the blade of his knife across his own throat to inform them of the method of their final execution.

Then he watched them die. He looked at his watch. Thirty seconds was what it took. Some things were the same the world over. He congratulated himself.

When he had asked Alain the time it had been 02.22h. It was now 02.29h. He rubbed his hands together and looked at the girl, her head twisted to the right and her body slumped almost demurely on it's side as if asleep. Pity, she would have been one hell of a lay.

After a moment's reflection he picked her up like a child and, holding her under one arm opened the rear door of his car with his right hand. He wasn't quite sure why but he had decided to dump her elsewhere to avoid any immediate connection with the other three corpses. He turned back to them.

He dragged Philippe on top of Delaunay and placed the man's knife in his hand. Then he plunged it into Delaunay's throat. He carefully cleaned his own knife and placed it in Delaunay's right hand. He cursed himself briefly for having slit both men's throats. Never mind, the police would still have to conclude that the three of them had killed each other in a fight. Josef chuckled. The mother of all fights for all three to be dead.

He decided to drive into the mountains. He felt elated but at the back of his mind he began a process of thought and strategic reformulation. Thomas had been wrong. The prostitution business was clearly not going to be a walkover. If the Côte d'Azur was going to be littered with corpses every time he fucked a whore what would happen when he tried to take over as king pimp?

He drove slowly up the Boulevarde Carnot and joined the motorway. The traffic was limited to a few juggernauts and he reached the slip road for Digne within a quarter of an hour. It was 02.55h. He looked round at the girl sprawled inertly in the back. What a waste. He laughed as he remembered an appalling English joke about necrophilia being a dead bore, turned back to concentrate on the road which was long and straight but heading for a dark mass which was the border of the southern Alps.

He began to relax. He enjoyed driving, appreciated the solitude and the sensation of being alone. Well, almost alone. The first corner appeared and within minutes the road was climbing rapidly. He drove for another hour, leaving Isola 2000 behind him and entered St. Etienne, just below Auron.

He drove through the village and started a steeper climb up the mountain behind. Another turn to the left and he was on a rough track leading down to an old quarry. Just like out of a bad movie he thought. He stopped the car and pulled the girl out. She was cold. The wind was quite strong and Havel shuddered slightly as the pine trees moved, their tips swinging across the glow of the moon and making the dim light flicker.

Plenty of stones. He carried the girl to the back of the quarry, stumbled and swore. He dropped her with distaste and stooped to pick up the closest stones. She was soon covered completely. Nothing to catch the eye, even if someone did venture down to this godforsaken spot.

He was in a hurry now to leave but imposed upon himself the time needed to smoke a cigarette. Control at all times. Essential.

Very tiresome. He had underestimated the situation. The word would get out. He would become a target. It seemed like he already was a target. Time to move on perhaps. Events seemed to be taking over. He could feel it. It didn't worry or frighten him, it just meant his remarkable mental and physical machine had to change gear and direction.

Josef flicked away his cigarette and climbed back into his car, settled back behind the steering wheel to enjoy the drive back and the view as the dawn light imperceptibly strengthened.

# AMRA

%

AMRA ARRIVED at Nice station at 10.00h on Saturday morning. She carried a small overnight bag and wore simple clothes. A pair of jeans, a white T-shirt and sandals. She could have passed unnoticed in the crowds jostling around the platform and queuing for the escalator up to the main hall. But her almost perfect oval face, her green eyes and trim but full figure attracted many a lustful glance. She radiated good health and carried a discreet odour of simple but pleasant eau-de-toilette.

She was tempted to get a taxi but decided against it. Faruk had told her that he wasn't going to start work until 12.30h and that he could wait until 12.15h. She knew the Niçois bus system perfectly and waited patiently for the N° 9 which would take her to Boulevard Pasteur, from where she could walk to the studio.

She sniffed the city's air and took in the familiar mixture of exhaust fumes, coffee, cooking, flowers and human sweat. Nice smelled like Nice and Strasbourg smelled like Strasbourg. That's just the way it was.

By the time she got off the bus, it was 10.30h. She walked down the hill going past the Pasteur hospital, turned left into the overbuilt "HLM" area and within 10 minutes was in front of Faruk's building. She was surprised not to see his motorbike but thought no more of it. She was excited, trembling with anticipation and joy at seeing her brother again.

She let herself in the main door with the keys she had kept from the days when they lived together in the studio and took the lift, now temporarily working again, up to the 5th floor. With her bag over her shoulder and clutching a little bunch of flowers, she stood in front of the door which was open a few inches.

She pushed it further ajar and let herself in, puzzled.

The studio was empty and lifeless. There was an overturned chair and broken glass on the floor and a strong smell of aniseed. There was a profound silence, the sort of quiet which emanated from abandonment. There were no vibrations of recent occupation, no way she could imagine Faruk having popped out to buy some cigarettes, no way she could imagine his imminent return. She knew it was all terribly wrong.

She stared out of the window, fear and dread rising uncontrollably. Without thinking, she moved across the room, the glass crunching under her feet, and opened the window. The flower pot was there, apparently undisturbed. She lifted it in and overturned it on the table. The two plastic bags were there. Maybe Faruk hadn't tried anything stupid, maybe he was at work. Maybe she was just reacting hysterically. Maybe this was just some kind of weird burglary.

She rinsed the bags, dried them and tucked them into her little case. Then she righted the chair, swept up the glass, washed up a few glasses and made Faruk's bed. She placed the flowers in one of the glasses on the centre of the table. She felt lonely, more lonely than she'd ever felt in her life.

As she stood in the middle of the room wondering what to do, quietly crying, the telephone rang. She picked up the receiver and just managed to say hello.

"This is George. Are you Faruk's sister?"

She remained silent for a few seconds and nodded without speaking.

"Hello, Amra? Are you there? That is Amra, is it?"

"Yes, I'm Amra."

"Look, I think you'd better come to 'Le Yacht'. I'm sorry, there's been an accident. I think you should come here right away. Do you want me to come and get you? I'll get a taxi."

"What accident?" She could manage no more than a whisper.

"Amra, I can't talk about this on the phone. Please don't ask me for details. Please."

"Just tell me. Is it bad? Is he alive?"

George drew in his breath, let it out slowly. "Faruk's had a bad motorcycle accident. The police are here. We're all devastated. We will all do whatever we can to help, Amra". There was another long pause. "Will you wait there, please? I'm coming."

Amra screamed into the phone. "A bad motorbike accident? Faruk? How bad?"

George tried to find the right words. "Amra, he's alive but unconscious. He's in a coma. I think you should see him as soon as possible."

Amra swayed as she registered the true meaning of his last words. George thought he was going to die, very soon.

"That wasn't an accident! That was not an accident! They tried to murder him. I know it! I know who did it!"

George was stunned. This had to be hysteria. The pitch and intensity of her voice were unbearable. The girl sounded temporarily insane. He decided to ask the police to send a car round for her.

"Amra, I can understand what you feel. Really. Please don't move. Somebody will come to pick you up in ten minutes. You mustn't go out."

Amra slammed the phone down and howled, inconsolable and drained. When the police arrived she was sitting in a trance at the table. They gently led her to the police station where George and Detective Alain Legrand were waiting for her.

⁄⁄⁄

Amra's state of shock lasted several hours. She was shuffled in and out of Legrand's office in the Maréchal Foch commissariat three times before she managed to speak, although she already unders-tood. She was on her own, on a ledge, the world was passing by, she didn't count any more. This was not a nightmare. Yes, it was a nightmare. There was no difference between dream and reality, pain and pleasure, song or silence, night or day. Was she alive?

Something moved in her brain. An outside look at herself. She was thinking in clichés. And the fact she saw this meant she was not dead, just detached from the outside world. But she wan-ted to be dead. How can you die when you can't even find the energy to kill yourself? This was worse than hell. This was para-lysis. Find the fire, find the hate, find them, find Racik. Yes. And find the courage to sit by her dying brother's bedside to bid him a final farewell.

"Mademoiselle Amra." It was Legrand. "You have all our sym-pathy. You are shocked. This is normal. We are sorry you had to be interviewed by us first, your friend informed us you suspected attempted murder. Now you must come to the St. Roch hospital and see your brother. Then we can open the investigation. Please, Mademoiselle Amra, not for me, for your brother."

Amra fought her paralysis. Stupid bloody cop. Didn't even know her, or Faruk. He didn't care. How could she soften to his words? How many other corpses, how many other bereft relatives had he faced? Look at him. He was tired. Bags under his eyes. He wanted to get back home, or move on to the next case. He wanted a simple solution. No complications. This was just ano-ther dossier. He was a bureaucrat. A file neatly filed and sealed and archived was better than a file open on his desk with a hundred different questions and no answers.

And yet, somehow, his words got through to her. Somehow she knew she had to leave her chair, move. The agony of immobility was too much and Legrand was showing her the way, giving her ersatz sympathy, leading her to the next step. Maybe that was what she feared most. Even more than what had happened, it was what was going to happen. The emptiness.

She hauled herself up, pulling on the edge of the grey table, nodded and said *"Allons-y."*

George took her arm, Legrand heaved a half-stifled sigh of relief and all three moved out into the linoleum floored corridor where a blue-clad driver awaited.

It was only 300 metres to the hospital. They could have walked up Rue Rothschild but Legrand seemed to want to use a driver. On the way, Amra nearly stifled on her vomit. Legrand watched, his eyes rinsed lifeless from his work and the alcohol he used as an anaesthetic. He gave her a handkerchief.

# STORM

///

HUGE BLACK CLOUDS massed on the Alps behind Menton and started scudding westwards over Monaco and above Nice where they swirled, hesitating before discharging. And as the rain began to spill down and the wind picked up, the tension over the city eased and the day's sins and detritus seemed to start to be washed away. Amra wept, Josef Havel slept, Lucas fretted and worried in his office, George phoned "Le Yacht" to say he would not be there until the next day, and Jérôme drove out of Nice along the coast-road on the first leg of his first trip to Liechtenstein, having decided not to take the motorway before stopping for half an hour in Monaco for a quick fling at the main casino. Absurd in a way when he had so much driving to do but irresistible.

The traffic was light and the roads were soaked. Above Villefranche he risked a glance at the sea below. Instead of its usual tranquil blue, the water was grey and whipped up and a massive white liner, ugly with its box-like superstructure, sat disconsolately in the middle of the bay. Cap Ferrat looked sad and dark.

Jérôme registered all of this in a second, but his heart was light and there was a song on his lips. His precious cargo was tucked in a cavity behind a welded plate in the boot of his Alfa Romeo. On the passenger seat was a carefully disordered jumble of maps, sunglasses, sandwich and half empty diet coke. He looked exactly like a tourist. This was a fun trip. He felt confident. Confident and rich.

Had his mind not been meandering around the globe seeking a suitable location for the villa he was going to buy as a surprise for his beloved wife, he might have noticed the black Mercedes in his rear-view mirror. He might have noticed how it had been behind him since he'd left the centre of Nice. He might have worried. But he didn't.

And as if these thoughts went through the mind of the driver behind him, the Mercedes fell back and allowed two cars to go in between it and Jérôme's. The little convoy arrived in Monaco and Jérôme made his way to the public underground car park opposite the Café de Paris. He smiled to himself as he drove past the municipal casino.

How about a handful of $100 bills, all on the number 17? His car entered the dimly lit car park. He found a space two floors down but continued down to the sixth level where there were only a dozen other vehicles. He got out of his car. He knew it was in complete security. He felt the tingle of excitement, the slight moistening of the palms of his hands. If his flutter was successful it would be a good omen for the Havel deal. Half an hour, in and out, and back on the road to Liechtenstein.

The Mercedes parked 50 metres away, not even noticed by Jérôme who had his back turned and was heading towards the lift. Thomas got out and followed him at a distance. As Jérôme took the lift, he ran up the stairs in time to see him leaving the shopping arcade at the top of the parking lot. He watched him stride towards the casino.

Thomas nodded approvingly. Havel had asked him to follow both Lucas and Jérome regularly, in particular Jérôme when "transport" days arrived, which he had insisted on being informed about. If out of superstition or simple gambling addiction Jérome was going to stop off at the casino before driving to Liechtenstein every time then there was no question about it. This was a perfect place to waylay him and snatch the money he was transporting: a no-man's land where Monte Carlo's ubiquitous cameras would not register anything abnormal. He would just get in the passenger side of Jérôme's car before he had time to get out, force him to drive out of Monaco.... The rest was going to be simple.

If Jérôme stopped off in Monaco regularly then the third or fourth time he would be waiting. If he didn't, he would find another spot to ambush him on the long road to Liechtenstein. He would take an advance on his commission and make out to Vuk that Jérôme had disappeared with the cash. He would have disappeared, of course, in the boot of the Mercedes before being buried in the mountains where he would never be found. But the money would be hidden elsewhere.

Thomas twitched with impatience. He needed some action, to push things forward. He was frustrated by Faruk's having killed himself. Still, the pig had been skewered. And this particular little piggy was going to have a swift, painless ending to his little piggy life.

His obsessive vision of a clean, white house on the cliffs of Crete, overlooking the Med, skimmed into his mind before he turned on his heel and walked back inside the car park.

///

Jérôme drove carefully for two and a half hours, pulled off the motorway at a filling station south of Milan and sat down at a table in the uncrowded restaurant next to it. The Alfa Romeo was parked outside, directly in view from his table. This was Italy, not Monaco.

He ordered pasta and mineral water and studied the map. He wasn't in a hurry, he would drive past Verona and up to Innsbruck. A bit circuitous but all motorway. Then he would branch off left, cross the border into Liechtenstein and left again to Vaduz. He calculated another six hours driving. He opened his case and studied the documents he had printed out from his internet search :

*At one time, the territory of Liechtenstein formed a part of the ancient Roman province of Raetia. For centuries this territory, geographically removed from European strategic interests, had little impact on European history. Prior to the reign of its current dynasty, the region was "enfieffed" to a line of the counts of Hohenems.*

" *Hohenems,*" he reflected. Sounded like something from Gulliver's travels.

*The Liechtenstein dynasty, from which the principality takes its name, comes from Castle Liechtenstein in faraway Lower Austria, which the family possessed from at least 1140 to the thirteenth century, and from 1807 onward. Schloss Vaduz, overlooking the capital, is still home to the prince of Liechtenstein.*

He felt intrigued. There was a Count Dracula quality to the whole thing. He speed-read, looking for something to attract his attention.

*Until the end of World War I, Liechtenstein first was closely tied to the Austrian Empire and later to Austria-Hungary; however, the economic devastation caused by WWI forced the country to conclude a customs and monetary union with its other neighbour Switzerland.*

Ah, there you go, landlocked Liechtenstein showing the first signs of going offshore!

*The Prince of Liechtenstein owns vineyards in Vaduz.*

Fascinating, Lucas would like to know about that.

*In the spring of 1938, just after the annexation of Austria into Greater Germany, eighty-four year-old Prince Franz I abdicated, naming his thirty-one year-old third cousin, Prince Franz Joseph, as his successor. While Prince Franz I claimed that old age was his reason for abdicating, it is believed that he had no desire to be on the throne if Germany were to gobble up Liechtenstein. His wife, whom he married in 1929, was a wealthy Jewish woman from Vienna, and local Liechtenstein Nazis had already singled her out as their anti-Semitic "problem". Although Liechtenstein had no official Nazi party, a Nazi sympathy movement had been simmering for years within its National Union party.*

Jérôme thought of Lucas' tirade about Switzerland. History, history, he could never get enough of it. Who knew all the connections between cause in one corner of Europe and effect in another? War between other countries leading to economic ruin in Liechtenstein, in turn prompting monetary union with Switzerland (which had its own relationship with the Nazis) ....

*In dire financial straits following the war, the Liechtenstein dynasty often resorted to selling family artistic treasures, including, for instance, the priceless portrait "Ginevra de' Benci" by Leonardo da Vinci, which was purchased by the National Gallery of Art of the United States in 1967.*

*Liechtenstein prospered, however, during the decades following, as it used its low corporate tax rates to draw many companies to the country.*

*The country's population enjoys one of the world's highest standards of living.*

Not surprising really, reflected Jérôme. Liechtenstein was one of the few countries in the world with more registered companies than citizens!

Easy Rules of Incorporation had induced about 75,000 holding (or so-called 'letter box') companies to establish nominal offices in Liechtenstein. Such processes provided about 30% of Liechtenstein's state revenue. Liechtenstein also generated revenue from the establishment of "Stiftungs" (Foundations), financial entities created to increase the privacy of non-resident foreigners' financial holdings. Foundations were registered in the name of a Liechtensteiner, often a lawyer.

*Recently, Liechtenstein has shown strong determination to prosecute any international money-laundering and worked to promote the country's image as a legitimate financial centre.*

Jérôme stopped reading and chuckled. Life was full of ironies. While Monaco, Jersey and Guernsey and others were squeaky clean in his view, he reckoned Liechtenstein still had a bit of work to do. He folded up his papers and walked back to the car. A black Mercedes was parked to one side of the restaurant. He didn't notice.

Six and a half hours later he was driving through the centre of Vaduz.

The Kunstmuseum, the future museum of modern and contemporary art in Vaduz was illuminated although it was not due to be completed until 1999/2000 when it would form a "black box" of tinted concrete and black basalt stone.

The streets were totally deserted. It was late. He looked at his watch. Just before midnight. He found his hotel, checked in, ordered a sandwich and a bottle of red wine to be sent up to his room. He was enjoying every minute. Tomorrow he would wander round the town, maybe see, if not visit, Vaduz Castle, Gutenberg Castle, the Red House and the ruins of Schellenberg before meeting Herr Teuber at Baransteitbank who would also introduce him to the attorney with power to sign on the account. Teuber had said the latter could be trusted; he was his cousin.

%

"'*Bankgeheimnis*' — bank secrecy — that may not stir the human soul, Jérôme, not the way '*Liberté, Egalité, Fraternité*' does, but it seems to work in Liechtenstein and that is good enough for me." Hans Teuber stared at Jérôme in as friendly a manner as his Germanic square face with its expressionless pale blue eyes permitted. He sat behind his desk and occasionally allowed his eyes to flicker in the direction of the large rucksack sitting beside Jérome's feet like an obedient dog.

"I agree, I approve entirely, I have no argument with you," replied Jérôme, slightly changing position in the armchair which placed him uncomfortably lower than Teuber. "I just never know how to justify my position, that offshore centres are intrinsically a good thing. I mean the basic function is to help people avoid tax which is illegal and can be construed as stealing. When people say that, it kind of foxes me because they are working with a different set of assumptions to myself."

Hans Teuber roared with what seemed slightly forced laughter. "My friend, I like you, I'm glad to put a face to a voice, Lucas always told me you were a good guy. Paying taxes is the responsibility of the customer, not the bank. That's the first point. But think about governments too, excluding places like Liechtenstein and Monaco which are labelled 'uncooperative' by all the other European governments because they set a bad example by encouraging freedom and work by low or inexistent taxes.

"Governments in general are quite simply thieves, they want it all. The little man, or the intelligent ones who seek to preserve what they have worked so hard for, are made to take the fall for the biggest mafias known to mankind.

"I've gone through many adjectives to describe the 'ruling class': statist, socialist, fascist all failed in some fundamental way to fully encompass what I was witnessing. Eventually, I chose the word "parasite" to describe these misbegotten elements of society because it is the most accurate scientific term available.

"When one steps back to look at the relationship between those in government (that's anyone getting a pay cheque from a government agency) and the remainder of society, one is naturally led to the parasite/host relationship.

"In biology, we know that there are beneficial parasitic organisms and there are detrimental organisms. But even the beneficial ones' existence can be detrimental to the host, generating one of two possible outcomes; the host suffers/dies or the parasites are eliminated.

" The very nature of government is to obfuscate its actions by so many layers of bureaucracy that even (especially?) those who are the ones to implement its machinations cannot see it. Those parasitic people now outnumber the hosts of modern pathological society. If they are not eliminated, the host dies. If the host retaliates it will be weakened and may die. However, if the host survives purging itself of its parasitic infestation it may survive to enjoy its existence a bit longer than it would have. It's not that there are tiny ravenous quantities of parasites that merely need to be inoculated against, but rather there are huge quantities of ravenous parasites feeding off dwindling hapless hosts.

"As to which laws we are morally obliged to obey, the law 'thou shalt not steal' is one of universal and unqualified application. Who is stealing here? The honest man who accumulates wealth or the government and its retinue of parasites that plunders half or more of an honest man's earnings?

"When the law has become perverted, it is not the moral obligation of citizens to accommodate it. Tax 'evasion' is a natural and morally healthy reaction. I can't see how trying to keep what one has honestly earned is immoral. So if Lucas says the money is not related to drugs or arms or anything distasteful like that and we are helping some victim to not be robbed, well, it's good enough for me. I consider it my duty to help."

It was Jérôme's turn to laugh. "God, I wish I had recorded that! It was brilliant. Great stuff, Hans. Anyway, now we know we are acting in a morally responsible manner can we put this in the safe please?"

Teuber registered the sarcasm, pressed a button on his telephone and asked his secretary to show in his cousin.

Jérôme stood up as Gerhardt Teuber walked in and felt an instant flash of dislike. The man looked slightly dissolute. Not really dirty, just grubby and out of condition. His handshake was reluctant and humid. Jérôme felt like wiping his own hand clean.

"Gerhardt acts as attorney on a number of accounts here and is experienced and discreet. He will look after you well. His fees are 2,000 Swiss Francs every quarter."

They chatted for a few minutes before setting off to the vaults of the bank, Jérôme explaining that a further $15,000,000 would be deposited, this being the first experimental trip. Gerhardt nodded, licking his lips nervously. Jérôme's antipathy increased.

One of the cashiers opened the main door to the vaults, behind which were a second set of doors made out of thick steel bars. Hans Teuber opened them with his own keys and asked the cashier to wait outside. They walked to the end of the strong room and Gerhardt produced a smaller key to a large safety deposit box, number 555. He opened it and gestured to Jérôme to place the cash inside. Jérôme stacked the $10,000 bundles at the back of the box, counting out loud until he reached the full amount, exactly $1,000,000.

The three men looked at each other, nodded, closed the door to the box and returned to the main banking hall. They shook hands and agreed to meet in about a week for the next instalment, before which time $200,000 of the cash would be deposited by Gerhardt into the company account.

Jérôme walked out to the brightly lit street and breathed in heavily. Baransteitbank and the Teubers had been having an increasingly claustrophobic effect on him. He needed to get back to the Côte d'Azur, see his children, eat and drink a glass of wine with his wife.

He set off. The Mercedes was no longer following him. Thomas had seen enough.

# GUEST

///

AMRA AND GEORGE stood in the forecourt of the hospital. Strangely, Amra was calmer now that she had seen her brother. Perhaps the fact that he was breathing had given her hope, the plethora of hospital equipment and the constant bleep from the cardio monitor. The doctor had told her the chances of survival were between zero and twenty per cent and if Faruk did survive he risked permanent physical and even mental handicap. But the recollection of Faruk's strength and vitality before the accident made it impossible for Amra to really believe this.

George observed her discreetly, not knowing what to say. She clutched a plastic bag with the few personal items that had been recovered. A residence and work permit, a wallet with some money and her picture in it, an insurance certificate and a mobile phone. Legrand had told George that the Kawasaki would have to be collected from the pound or sent to the scrap-heap. George said he would have it picked up.

They walked in silence to the Place Maréchal car park where George had left his brother's runabout, a Renault 5, and drove towards the station to look for a hotel.

It was already 19.00h. George was desperate for a drink. He couldn't leave Amra on her own. Even her little suitcase made him want to cry; it seemed so cheap and empty. The hotels looked cheap and empty, too. He didn't ask her, he simply told her that he was taking her back to his brother's flat for the night. They'd look for a hotel tomorrow.

He watched her out of the corner of his eye again, as he drove. She was magnificent. No make-up, shattered, bereft, exhausted. And magnificent. Her breasts swelled as she breathed and the roundness of her thighs and hips showed through her cotton skirt. George felt ashamed as he registered the familiar stirrings of desire. He forced his mind back to the situation they were facing.

When they arrived at Lucas' flat it was 19.30h and a warm glow of soft light and music greeted them as he opened the door. Lucas was sipping a large glass of whisky and his pretty little mistress, Chloé, was in the kitchen which adjoined the sitting room, open plan.

"Lucas, I'm helping out a friend, Amra. She's going to stay tonight, if you don't mind. She needs a bit of kip. I'll explain later."

Lucas got up with his glass in his hand, obviously not overcome with pleasure but making an effort to be courteous. "No problem, George. Delighted. You'd better have some spaghetti with us. Chloé, two more helpings please." He blew her a kiss.

*"Pas de problème, mon chéri."* Chloé deftly added water to the saucepan and put additional plates on the bar-cum-table. Amra asked if she could have a shower and George led the way to the bathroom. Lucas looked quizzically at his brother when he returned.

"So where did you find her then? Jesus, have you seen her tits? She's a cracker, George. Mind you, looks a bit sulky. Maybe you're not banging her hard enough."

"Piss off, Lucas. If you knew the full story you wouldn't talk like that."

"How can I know the full story, for God's sake? You've barely told me her bloody name. Anyway, you did say one night, yeah?"

George looked at Lucas with fleeting dislike. Then he realised he was actually being hospitable beyond the call of duty and his crude digs were not meant badly.

"Look, Lucas, the girl's brother is lying in hospital in a coma from which he will probably never emerge. We think he's going to die. He worked in 'Le Yacht' with me. She's wiped out and earlier on she was even delirious. She told me somebody had tried to murder him. Shock, I suppose. In fact, he came off his bike."

"Jesus wept". Lucas looked genuinely taken aback. "Well, this is going to be a fun supper, isn't it? I mean, what are we going to talk about?"

George knew this wasn't as callous as it sounded.

"Pretend I haven't told you anything. Don't tell Chloé, she hasn't overheard us." George relaxed a bit as he swallowed his whisky. He managed his first smile of the day.

"Just be your normal, charming self, Lucas."

# MESSAGE

IT WAS 04.00h, THREE DAYS ON. Amra was still staying at Lucas' flat. George's groans had awoken her. She was sleeping in the tiny bedroom next to his. She felt refreshed and swung her long legs out of the bed and put on the lamp. Her clothes were in a pile on the floor and her bag on the bedside table. In a few seconds she found her bearings, remembered where she was. Another groan.

She tiptoed to the door. There was a two metre corridor. Lucas' room was on the other side of the sitting room. George's door was perpendicular to her own. She put her ear against it and could hear heavy, sporadic breathing and the creaks of a bed. A picture of George making love fluttered through her mind. But then he groaned again, and it wasn't from pleasure. It was a drawn out cry of anguish.

She opened his door and the light from her room was enough for her to see him in his bed in a tangle of bedclothes, glistening with sweat. She entered the room hesitantly and watched him from the side of his bed for a full minute. This had to be more than a nightmare, his handsome features were contorted and he seemed to be fending off some violent enemy. Suddenly he relaxed and after a few seconds opened his eyes. His breathing became more regular and he groped for the light switch.

"Are you OK?" asked Amra, somewhat lost for words. She wanted to sit on his bed and press his hot face against her cool breasts, run her fingers through his hair.

George remained silent for a few seconds and then, wearily, "Yes."

"Shall I make you some tea?" He nodded gratefully and sat on the edge of his bed with his head in his hands. She saw he was wearing boxers and took in his surprisingly muscular chest and arms. George's daily workouts had evolved into heavy weight training and his youthful body had responded. Long rippling muscles showed on his arms and back and his shoulders were those of a powerful swimmer. All of his left flank, arm and leg were covered with relatively fresh scars and stitch marks. What had happened to the man?

They sipped their tea in the peace of the dawn and tacitly accepted their bond. She placed a hand on his, gently, and asked if he felt better.

"Don't even bother to worry about me. I'll tell you one day. Nightmares. They're worse since . . . since Faruk's accident, I mean, after what happened. I nearly got killed on my motorbike a few months ago and, well, I'll tell you another time."

George scratched his head awkwardly and then looked up. "Amra, what happened to your family?"

She looked back, momentarily stunned. The question went to the heart of everything. "Everyone is dead." She choked back her tears and felt the despair climb into her throat, felt the mutilation in her soul and knew there was only one thing that would give her life any meaning. Revenge. That would be her goal, her one and only motivation. She would plan her life exclusively around this. George would perhaps be her ally, but not her lover. Or if he was her lover, then a short-term one. She looked at his shoulders again.

A heavy silence fell upon them. The room seemed frozen, motionless as a photograph. Their breathing was barely audible and her hand felt cold and clammy on his. He dared not move until she withdrew it, after several minutes, and walked to the window, drawing open the curtains. Then she spoke evenly and flatly for twenty minutes. She told her story.

George heaved a deep, uneven sigh.

Amra walked slowly round behind his chair and back again. She sat down opposite and watched him as he stared at the floor.

"I've told you everything, George. And now you're going to tell me, not what you think about the war and humanity and suffering, but what you think about what's going on here and now and whether or not you can help. If you can't, it doesn't matter. If you don't believe what I say, it doesn't matter either. But I'm not leaving this town until I find the people who tried to murder Faruk." She paused.

" Make no mistake. It was the same people who tortured and raped my sister, slaughtered my parents. They're here in Nice. God knows how or why but the one who led the convoy, the bastard who was really responsible for what happened, he's here. Faruk called me and told me. And I've got a lead, George."

She paused again and then repeated almost inaudibly, "I've got a lead."

George lit a cigarette and, without thinking, poured himself a large glass of JB. He walked to the fridge and pulled out some ice. Staring at his drink, he swirled it around before swallowing it in one go and filling it again. Must run in the family he thought. Jesus, he was almost as bad as Lucas.

"You've listened to Faruk's messages?" he asked. Amra nodded. "Yes, I knew his access code. There's still a day left before they are wiped out. But it doesn't matter. I've written them down word for word. You wouldn't understand them anyway, they're in Bosnian. The only problem is I've only got the message, not the number."

"What about the numbers that Faruk stocked in his mobile?"

"He never used the option. I guess he only had a few numbers to remember."

George lit another cigarette and asked her what the message was.

"The message was this. I can tell you by heart: ' Faruk, you're right. He's here. We've checked and put a tail on him. We've got to be careful. See you at the usual place and time and we'll get this sorted. We're with you Faruk, but only if it's really thought out. There could be others.'"

George raised his eyes and stared at her. "Amra, I know what the usual place is and I know what the usual time is. There's a bar in the old town where Faruk met his mates after work. We can go together if you want. I'll help you, Amra, but this is beginning to feel like a bad movie. What are you really intending to do? You can't kill this guy, even if you find him."

"Why not?" Amra smiled for the first time.

"Amra, this is not how real life works. You don't gun people down, you don't risk going to prison for the rest of your life, you . . . you . . . go to the police." George felt the emptiness of his words and his voice trailed off.

She said quietly, "Real life? Please don't tell me about real life. You may have a real life. I don't and my family has no life at all. Life has stopped for them and for me, George. You can understand that. Just take me to the bar. Take me to Saleh and his friends. I can look after the rest. I'll do it my way, the only way, but your involvement stops at the bar."

George laughed suddenly. "Yeah, of course."

Amra allowed herself a wry smile. A glass vase, half full of sand, stood on the coffee table next to her. A slightly uncharacteristic item of decoration which Lucas had been given by a girl-

friend of yesteryear. She put one beautiful hand inside and scoo-
ped up some of the sand. Then she watched it sift through her
parted fingers.

"Time might be running out for Vuk Racik," she whispered.

# ACCELERATE

JÉRÔME DROVE BACK contentedly towards Nice after his third trip to Liechtenstein, stopping for coffee at Villefranche. Once in Nice he parked in the Rue Alberti as usual and took the lift up to the 5th floor, then walked briskly into the bank. Lucas was waiting for him nervously. He was not in sparkling form. He had argued stupidly with one of the directors from Geneva and even sworn at one of the staff. This was totally out of character.

"How did it go?"

Jérôme feigned disappointment and fear.

"You've no idea . . . ." he paused for dramatic effect as he clamped his hand to his forehead, but seeing how tense and worried Lucas was looking he continued quickly, "how well it went! Dumped the money with Fritz, left instructions with that creep Gerhardt to credit another $200,000 to the company account, came back. No hitches, Lucas. What's eating you? Where's your panache, your carefree muddling through? I reckon you've got women problems. Either that or you're getting old."

Lucas poured himself a drink, not the first of the day, lit another cigarette and sat back heavily in one of the leather armchairs. He didn't want to communicate his fear to Jérôme. Ever since George had voiced his own suppressed thoughts about Josef Havel he had been getting more and more worried, drinking absurd amounts of JB and losing sleep.

He felt, he knew that something was profoundly wrong and that the Havel business was leading him way out of his depth.

Nightmarish visions of prison, scandal . . . but Havel had him like a rabbit in his headlights. He couldn't move out of the way. He was frightened. More than frightened. He was beginning to panic. He kept his voice level however.

"Jérôme, you reassure me. You make everything sound so simple. You know I'm a bit of a worrier. I just think this is so big, this deal, I sometimes feel it simply can't work."

Jérôme looked at him and felt some of his exuberance drain away.

"We're in it up to our ears now, so there's no going back. Listen, I've made three successful trips so far. The money is in the safe and each time I go, $200,000 are credited to the account. I've had no problems. Nobody follows me, nobody bothers me. Gerhardt is just one more client going down to the vault once a week.

"Look, I'll speed it up if you want. Is it really logical to take $1,000,000 dollars per trip? If I get stopped, what's the difference between one and four million, for example? Let's get the bloody thing over with. There's $13,000,000 left. I'll do it in three trips. We'll have finished in a few weeks. 15th July, that's our objective. After that we get our commission, the signatures are changed and Havel takes over. We'll be out of the whole thing and we'll be rich. What's so bad about that?"

Lucas swallowed yet another large neat shot of JB and felt slightly better.

"Yeah, you're right. Let's get it over with. I just hope we never hear of or see Havel again when you've finished. He gets up my nose. I don't even dare check out that second hand car business stuff. I reckon it's all bullshit. He got his money somewhere else. Where, is the question?"

Jérôme nodded. "I've checked, Lucas. Sorry, but I can't reassure you this time. There was no car dealership, there was no sale. And there was no Josef Havel. I didn't want to tell you because there was no point. So? We're laundering money on a massive scale. But that was obvious pretty early on. You seem to want to hide these things from yourself. You like to worry but you don't like to see clearly what you're worrying about. We're taking a risk and it's too late to hedge our bets or back out. Stop drinking and we'll cope a lot better."

Lucas rubbed his forehead and looked away. Jérôme left his office and he delved into his briefcase. After a minute of fumbling he found what he wanted and started reading where he had left off what seemed so long ago.

*IN GENERAL, PROBLEM DRINKING QUALIFIES AS ALCOHOLISM WHEN THE PERSON:*

- *drinks compulsively.*
- *keeps drinking in spite of adverse consequences.*
- *gets upset when alcohol is not readily available.*

*THE KEY ELEMENTS OF ANY ADDICTION, WHETHER CHEMICAL OR BEHAVIOURAL ARE:*

- *Compulsivity- meaning loss of control over the behaviour - i.e. continuing to engage in a particular behavior after repeated attempts to stop.*
- *Continuation despite adverse consequences, such as loss of job, money, marriage, or health - or arrests or public humiliation.*
- *Preoccupation or obsession with obtaining and using the substance or participating in the behavior to the detriment of other essential life activities or goals*

*Addictions are defined not by how much of the drug or behaviour is used, but rather the effects on the person's life. An addiction can be suspected when the behaviour has made the person's life unmanageable.*

*As their disease progresses, alcoholics need to drink more and more often, just to feel normal. Increasingly, they realise that once they start to drink, they can't stop. Yet they desperately want to keep from getting drunk, both to avoid embarrassment and unpleasant withdrawal symptoms such as trembling, irritability, nausea, or insomnia. No strategy works for long, however. Inwardly disgusted with themselves, alcoholics vacillate between anger and depression. Personal relationships deteriorate. Job performance suffers.*

*In addition, physical problems develop. Alcoholics suffer from disturbing memory lapses called blackouts. Feeling edgy and anxious, some may experiment with and become addicted to tranquilizers. Alcoholics eat poorly, because their irritated liver and inflamed digestive system give them heartburn, nausea, and gas. Sex drive dwindles. Insomnia robs them of needed sleep...*

Fuck, how much of this was true? Was he losing control? Was he making love less often? Chloé hadn't said anything but then she wouldn't. She was like a lot of women in his experience, they loved having good sex but could survive for ages without it.

But he was drinking more and earlier and he had to admit it was to forget problems.....the problem.....and he had to admit that as soon as he stopped drinking the problem was still there, bigger and heavier and uglier.

A vision of Havel's face floated in front of him, its features contorted with laughter as it contemplated his gradual loss of dignity.

# ON THE TRAIL

FARUK'S FRIENDS, Ahmed and Saleh, had lost no time in following up on his information. The inner group of Bosnian refugees in Nice was composed of at least twelve men who were quickly and efficiently fanned out over the centre of Nice on the lookout for a black Mercedes with Italian number plates and a new Audi with 06(Nice) plates. They waited outside the town's main restaurants and bars in the evenings. Their speed of reaction had enabled them to spot Havel going into the Negresco bar with a girl just a few days after being tipped off.

Three motorcycles and one car (which was all they had between them) were parked around the hotel within ten minutes. One of the motorcyclists had waited in the Rue du Congrès near the exit of the bar, another 100 metres from the front of the hotel and the third on the promenade between the hotel and the sea. The driver of the car had waited on the other side of the hotel.

Havel had emerged from the front entrance on the corner of the Promenade des Anglais and walked casually with the girl in the direction of the Casino Ruhl before hailing a taxi, unaware of his four observers who took it in turns to stay behind the taxi which drove to St Laurent du Var, the little port a few kilometres west of Nice. Havel had got out at the entrance to the port and entered one of the restaurants with his companion. He reappeared at midnight, boisterous and slightly drunk. He was alternately squeezing the girl's neck and bottom and was clearly warmed up for a night of pleasure.

He was followed back to the luxury furnished apartment he had initially rented through Bergé (and still kept despite his move to Antibes) on the corner of Place Masséna, a few hundred metres from the opera house and the old Nice. From that moment on he was tailed, every movement noted.

A day later, Saleh had followed him to his new abode on the Cap d'Antibes where Havel had rented accommodation from Eric Bergé again, to whom he had explained that the purchase of the villa would have to be delayed pending receipt of funds. It was noted that his friend Thomas had moved to a small hotel in Avenue des Fleurs, a kilometre from the centre of Nice.

The only thing that Saleh and his friends could not understand was why Faruk had failed to respond to their news immediately. They had left a message on his mobile 48 hours after locating Havel, not wishing to provoke the impatient Faruk into immediate action which might jeopardise their success so far and scare off their prey. But four days had now gone by and they telephoned "Le Yacht." The manager sounded strange, hesitated, and then told them the news.

That evening, the three friends, Saleh, Ahmed and Edmond, were staring morosely into their beer glasses at "Thor's", oblivious to the music and excitement around them, when George and Amra came to their table. They knew Amra, but hadn't seen her for two years.

All three registered how she had changed. The slightly adolescent looking, underdeveloped slip of the girl of yore had been replaced by a magnificent woman with shapely hips and full breasts. Her hair was longer and she stood with unselfconscious confidence by the table. Not a man, or woman, in the bar had failed to notice her.

Saleh felt his throat tighten and his breathing shorten. Saleh had loved Faruk as a brother and used to joke and flirt innocently with Amra when he'd met her in Nice before. But something deeper stirred in him as he took her hand and kissed her on the cheek. The others greeted George and kissed Amra warmly. After simple tearful condolences there was a silence followed by a collective sigh. After a minute Amra looked up at them.

"It's good to see you again, Faruk's friends," she said. "He often talks about you. I've managed to find you thanks to George here and the message you left on the mobile. I know who you were talking about. I know who "he" is. He is the man who murdered my family and he's the man who has tried to murder Faruk."

The four men looked at each other, waiting to see who would speak first. Saleh replied.

"Vuk Racik. He's one of the worst. And he's one of the most dangerous. We know what he did in Bosnia. Faruk told us about your family. But we understand . . . we understand .... Faruk's condition was caused by a genuine motorcycle accident. That's to say that Faruk knew about Racik's presence in Nice, but Racik couldn't have known about Faruk's."

"Listen Saleh. Listen, all of you. There is no way Faruk found out about Racik and then just happened to fall off his motorbike." She paused, closing her eyes as she felt the tears welling up. Then she channelled the hate and anger back into her brain and regained control. "Coincidences like that don't happen. Not when Racik is involved. One way or another he's behind it. One way or another it was an attempted assassination, disguised as an accident. Now, please, tell me what you know."

There was a lull in the music and they dropped their voices. A blonde waitress appeared at the table and they ordered drinks. Saleh explained everything they had accomplished, hesitating every time he mentioned Faruk's name. He indicated the location of the apartments on a map of Nice and Antibes and told Amra how Vuk's nighttime sorties were now centred on Cannes, particularly the luxury hotels where discreet high class whores could be picked up in the piano bars. He described the new Audi Vuk had bought and he described their preliminary plans for killing him.

"That's it, Amra. That's what we know and that's what we've planned so far."

Amra nodded her head but she couldn't absorb their tentative plans, nor could she wait. She had no time. Her revenge had to be terrible and it had to be done by her and her alone. Live by the sword, die by the sword. She wanted the taste of revenge in her mouth, desperately. She just had to put the wheels in motion. This couldn't be left to Saleh and his cronies. Softies, all of them. Nothing would stop her. She wanted to slice, to cut. She knew what Vuk treasured most. What any man treasured most. She snapped her teeth shut and, pretending to sip her drink, spat violently.

Her beer foamed and spilt onto her lap. Saleh immediately stood up, proffering a paper napkin but she waved him away, managing a laugh. "Sorry, I haven't done that for ages. I swallowed the wrong way. Oh, God, it's gone up my nose."

Everybody settled back and the tension eased away. Amra's laugh made them feel better. Only George was puzzled. He felt he knew her intimately now. Intimately enough to know that behind this little pantomime lurked something dangerously out of control.

"One thing," said Saleh, tentatively. " Faruk. I went to see him today. I swear to you, his hand moved."

Amra and George looked at each other.

"Tomorrow morning, Amra. Not now. We'll see him tomorrow."

# ALIVE

IT WAS 8.00H the following morning. Amra took George's hand and led him along the hospital corridor. They were accompanied by a nurse.

"The doctor will be here for you to consult after you have seen your brother, Mademoiselle." The nurse spoke respectfully. "He'll tell you what he thinks. I know what I think: it's a miracle. He moved his hand yesterday and opened his eyes for a few seconds. Around 20.00h when his friend was here. Then he went back to sleep. But it wasn't a comatose sleep. He moved fractionally a lot of the time. There was expression on his face. That's what I must warn you about. The expression. He looks deeply traumatised, even when he is sleeping. Something is troubling him, something that goes beyond the accident in my view."

George looked at her. All of 45 years old, no doubt about that, but her crisp white uniform showed off her fullness and anyway, George had always fantasised about nurses. There was something about their authority, mixed in with their implicit kindness and the fact they had right of access to all one's intimacy. This one was a superior version. He flicked his attention back to what she was saying.

"He may not have registered the actual accident in his mind yet. Anyway, you know him. You can talk to him even if he appears to be asleep. He may be too tired to open his eyes but still be able to hear you."

Amra nodded her head and George squeezed her hand. Neither knew what to expect. The nurse asked them to slip on sterilised plastic shoe covers and paper overalls. They pushed open the door to room 261 and entered silently. There was a subdued glow from the light above the bed, like an emergency light in an underground station, and the somehow familiar quiet beeping of the cardio monitor.

Faruk lay on his back, his head in bandages, the rest of his body covered by a sheet, except for his left arm which had the drip feed. Transparent plastic tubes protruded from each nostril.

Amra sat by his bed and tentatively touched his arm. Then she started stroking it to the rhythm of her sobs. After a few minutes she took control of herself and studied Faruk's face. The nurse was right, it had expression, even a frown, and the message was one of profound frustration.

"George," she whispered, "He's thinking, his brain is working. He's thinking about Vuk Racik and how he can't kill him because he's paralysed in bed. He's thinking how he came so close to revenge. He's thinking he might lose him, never be able to move again. It's unbearable for him."

George switched his eyes from Amra to Faruk and looked more closely at him. He had no doubt she was right.

"Do you think he can hear us now? Do you think he's really sleeping or just unable to move?"

Amra looked down at her brother's hand which seemed strong even though his arm seemed, already, slightly emaciated.

"Faruk my love, can you hear me? Will you understand if I talk to you? Are you ......are you OK?" What a ridiculous question. "Can you move your finger?"

There was a moment's silence. A minute almost imperceptible shudder ran through Faruk's body. After a few seconds he raised his index finger about half a centimetre.

Amra grimaced in an effort to hold back her tears again. Then she sobbed and laughed alternately.

"I knew it. I knew it. You can hear me! You can understand me. Faruk, my baby brother, I'm here, I'm here with George. George from "Le Yacht", you remember him don't you?"

Faruk's frown relaxed slightly and he raised his finger again. George spoke.

"I'm here alright. I'm here my friend. I'm looking after your sister, so you have nothing to worry about. You're going to get better, you're already getting better. And we're going to see you every day, every single day until you get up and walk out of this place. It's good to be with you again, Faruk."

"Can I go on talking, Faruk?" Amra watched his finger. Again, a tiny movement. She started talking again, calmly now and with confidence.

"OK Faruk, listen my brother. What I have to say is easy to understand and it's true and it's what you want to know more than anything else. I've found our enemy and he will soon be dead. It was your friends, Saleh and the others, who located him, thanks to you, and they told me. They have been following him and they know his movements and his filthy habits. He can't even breathe without them knowing about it. They even watched him kill four people in Cannes."

Faruk didn't move his finger but his total immobility did not disguise the fact he was listening. In fact it made him look even more attentive.

"They are going to look after his departure from this planet and send him to hell full of bullet holes. And they're not going to make it easy for him. He's going to go with the pain he deserves. They will be remorseless.

"Sleep easy, Faruk, sleep with the knowledge that our nightmare is coming to an end and it's all thanks to you. You and I are going to be free, freer than we've ever been, to live."

The frown eased again. The finger twitched. Faruk went back to sleep.

# IN LOVE

THE FOLLOWING EVENING Josef Havel stood in his Antibes apartment and looked across from the Cap d'Antibes to the walls of the old city. A low table in the middle of the room was littered with bottles and overflowing ashtrays. He had just ushered out his favourite prostitute. Favourite because he had taken her back to his new home twice in the same week.

He stared at the debris and then at himself in the reflection from the window. He did not feel good. He felt empty and dissatisfied. He couldn't understand why his money and his freedom, which had acquired for him unlimited access to champagne and whores, did not make him feel better. What the hell was missing?

He showered and drove his car into Cannes. He avoided the "Tonga." And while he was sitting on the terrace of the Majestic, watching some frivolous overweight tourists splash around in the immaculate pool, he suddenly realised what it was that had been eluding him.

She was on her own, a dark haired angel dressed in white. She was undeniably the most beautiful woman he had ever seen. He forgot his visceral aversion to anyone not part of the supreme white race. He forgot his boredom, his listlessness and his past and his present. He even forgot his champagne. She was a work of art that sent shivers up his spine and chivalrous fantasies into his mind and his heart. Josef Havel was in love.

He watched her until she was obliged to look up. A small neutral smile. She sat back with a magazine on her lap and seemed to sigh. And the sigh seemed to say to Josef Havel that it was stupid for two young people on their own not to introduce themselves. He waved over the waiter. Please ask that lady if she will accept a glass of champagne. She looked amused and flashed a smile which a more sensitive man might have questioned. But Josef Havel couldn't believe his luck. He walked over, timid but determined, like a schoolboy. She gestured that he could take a seat. Amra's dark eyes flashed with the full force of her hatred and revulsion. Josef Havel found them charming. She bared her teeth like a wild animal. Josef Havel found her smile captivating.

The trap was set.

"Hi, my name's Josef, Josef Havel. It's a nice evening."

Amra's jaw tightened. She forced herself to look into the man's eyes and felt the bile released into her guts. She was unable to proffer her hand. Havel found this shyness so sweet.

"Amparo.Amparo Jimenez." she improvised. "Yes, it's a nice evening. Are you on holiday? Are you staying at the hotel?"

Amra's French accent was almost perfect but she had decided to say she was Spanish. The chances of Racik, or Havel as he called himself, speaking any Spanish were minute, whereas she could speak it passably and also talk knowledgeably about Spain. Who cared? This was all going to be over soon anyway. She felt the solid weight of her handbag against her foot.

Josef relaxed and started his well-rehearsed story. He could see from the way she stayed quiet and listened attentively, nodding her head, that she was interested in everything he said. He ordered a fresh bottle of champagne, crossed his long muscular legs and felt happy and confident.

What's more, he thought, Spanish was OK. That explained the olive skin and the almost black hair. Christ, she was so gorgeous he wouldn't mind bedding her if she was an Arab or, worse, a Bosnian Muslim. The latter he had raped but not, according to his criteria, properly bedded. Half his mind was imagining her thighs and what she would look like when they opened in front of him, the other half concentrated on his story.

The light dimmed as the evening wore on and the pool was emptied of bathers. Amra watched her prey like a cat and calculated. How long before she could kill this revolting bit of human detritus? Why not this evening? She could ask for a lift back to her hotel and shoot him as soon as he stopped his car at traffic lights. She could......slow down, slow down. No mistakes, no precipitation.

Josef talked on. She decided to leave, give him her number - he was sure to ask for it - and see what he suggested.

# UGLY

JÉRÔME MET LUCAS at 8.00h in the bank before the rest of the staff came in. The previous evening they had removed $4,000,000 from the vault and placed it quite simply behind the sofa in Lucas' office. The alarm system was so sophisticated that neither worried about security and in any event neither of them had independent access to the vault. Lucas could get the second key if he wanted (duplicates of all keys were kept with the Crédit Agricole) but Solange, Lucas' secretary and the bank's Girl Friday, who handled the occasional cash transaction and transfers, was the only person with the combination.

Both key and combination were needed and even Lucas couldn't get the combination from Solange. It was too deeply ingrained from her training that no one, not even the manager, could be allowed to share the number. If she were to literally disappear, he would have to call senior administration in Geneva.

They always separated the two events – Lucas requesting access to the vault and removing something, and Jérôme leaving with a small suitcase – so that the latter took place without curious glances from the staff, one of whom might make a connection. When the staff came in at 8.30am they would have forgotten the first event and not witnessed the second.

The vault or strong room itself housed signature cards, private client documents such as property deeds and wills, account opening documentation for Geneva and Luxembourg and the main cash safe. Cash was transferred to the day safe and returned every evening. Havel's cash was stashed in a separate metal filing cabinet to which only Lucas had the key. The original suitcase, the size of a trunk, had been thrown out.

Jérôme had often worried him about the possibility of an internal audit but he had shrugged this off given that the last one had taken place in January and, as he said, lightning never struck twice in the same place in the same year. Havel's cash was neatly separated into $1,000,000 parcels.

Jérôme placed two rucksacks on the floor in Lucas' office and filled them with the four parcels. He was dressed informally in jeans and sneakers and a white T-shirt. He was brisk and efficient and told Lucas he would see him for lunch in the Félix Faure the following day after the trip to Liechtenstein was completed.

"Are you sure everything's OK?" asked Lucas.

"Got the money, got a car, arranged a meeting with our friend, Mr Power of Attorney – yes, everything's OK. See you at 12.30h tomorrow. Set up a beer for me. I think I'm going to be feeling thirsty." He waved goodbye.

Jérôme's good mood stayed with him. All the way to Monaco. His trips to the casino had indeed become something of a superstitious routine and he had kept on winning. Money made people dream and he was as much a dreamer as anyone. As much as Thomas, with his Cretian cliffs and little white house with a window looking out on the Mediterranean, fig trees in the foreground and fishing boats moving imperceptibly across the horizon. As much as Lucas, who imagined himself sitting idly on a terrace in an old bastide in the hills of Châteauneuf de Grasse, sipping a glass of rosé while he watched Chloé's lovely bottom as she moved amongst the fruit trees.

Perhaps more than Vuk, who so far had never dreamed of anything except chasing pussy and drinking as much fine champagne as possible - until his recent romantic encounter of course.

Jérôme dreamed of the surprise for his wife when he bought tickets for her and the children to join him on a trip to Costa Rica. And when they arrived at the airport at San José, the chauffeur waiting for them, the beautiful drive to Tamarindo, the house on the beach where the giant turtles came to lay their eggs and the Pacific stretched out before them, the thunder of the surf and the children squealing with joy in the sand, the tropical flora and the pure, untainted wine, the music, the surfers . . . .

He switched his attention back to the road, as he turned off at Cap Ferrat to take a short cut past the Beaulieu casino and continue on his way to Eze, Cap d'Ail and the entrance to Monaco.

The traffic slowed to a crawl and virtually stopped just before the port of Monaco. He glanced up at the Palace on the right and smiled to himself. Maybe Prince Rainier, Princess Caroline and Stéphanie, Prince Albert would like to have some time off from affairs of state and come and stay in his house on the beach. Amazing where your mind could go when you let it wander.

After some twenty minutes he arrived at La Place du Casino. He felt thirsty. As soon as he'd left the carpark he would go for a beer in the Café de Paris. Then he would allow himself another half hour in the casino. He started the descent into the municipal car park under the gardens, feeling totally relaxed, even drowsy. Was it really sensible always to go down to the sixth level? What did he really gain in terms of security? It just felt better. The more he burrowed, the less likely the predators . . . what predators?

He smiled again and nosed his car into a slot. As usual, there were plenty of spaces free on this level. In fact, there was only one car, a Mercedes, parked next to the stairwell. He stretched, switched off the ignition.

There was the familiar sound of the centralised locking system on his car being released as he opened his door. Within a second, Thomas wrenched open the passenger door and pointed a lethal looking black revolver at him, pulling him viciously back into his seat by the hair.

"Not a squeak, not a movement. Just listen. Got me?" Thomas climbed in and threw a large empty rucksack onto the back seat.

Jérôme stared with horror at the man. His stomach churned and his bowels went liquid. This was his worst nightmare come true, not something he had ever imagined possible. He recognised Thomas after a few seconds. He'd seen him with Josef Havel on several occasions.

"Start the car again and drive out of the car park. Here's the money to pay at the exit. I wouldn't want you to be out of pocket. Oh, and by the way, your children will be all right if you don't do anything stupid."

Jérôme froze. His breathing turned into little stabbing snatches at the stale air in the car. He could just whisper "What do you mean . . . my children?"

Thomas looked at him with disgust. "Just get control of yourself and, like I told you, everything will be fine and dandy. Now, either you start this fucking car and do what I say or you and your little family aren't going to be boring me any longer. You know what I mean. Get moving."

Jérôme regained a minimum of mobility in his limbs and started the car. He reversed and then moved jerkily forwards, keeping to the right as he climbed the winding exit out of the car park.

Thomas prodded him violently in the ribs with the revolver as they emerged into the bright sunlight of the casino square and ordered him to follow the signposts to the motorway in the direction of Ventimiglia. Within 20 minutes they had driven through La Turbie and exited onto the A8.

As Thomas expected, they were waved through the customs control at the border by drowsy looking Carabinieri. Jérôme was told to drive towards Col de Tende. Vintimiglia sprawled to the right of them and then behind as they headed north. After driving a mere 20 kilometres they were already in rugged, mountainous countryside. Thomas pointed to a track leading off the main road and down to a rock strewn river.

"This is where we say goodbye, young man. You walk down to the river and count to a hundred and then you can start walking back home. I'm borrowing the car if you don't mind. Just explain where the money is would you? "

Jérome considered his options and decided he didn't have any. He opened the boot of the Alfa, Thomas standing at a safe distance, pointing the revolver at his head. He pulled back the carpet, took out the spare wheel and gave a panel at the back a sharp punch with the side of his hand. It snapped back neatly and revealed the two rucksacks with the four parcels.

"Not bad for an amateur, not bad at all," grunted Thomas.

As Jérôme turned towards the river, Thomas kicked him hard in the back and he staggered towards the water. The last thing he remembered was the exquisite agony of the two bullets that ripped into his back. He fell into the water and was out of sight within seconds. Thomas watched with idle curiosity, wondering where the body would be washed up. It would certainly get caught in the rocks and not get discovered for weeks, maybe months.

Keeping his gloves on, as he had from the start, he transferred the four parcels to his larger rucksack, got into the car and headed back to Ventimiglia. He parked the car next to the station and, ticket already prepared, rucksack in hand, walked calmly onto the train which would leave him in Monaco in 15 minutes. He looked at his watch and smiled again. God, things were simple. Now, a quick call to Vuk to say the little French piggy had disappeared, pick up his car and back home to count the money. There had to be well over a million, he was sure of it.

Crete seemed closer than ever. But Vuk would have to be disposed of first. Another smile crossed his normally expressionless face as he watched the Mediterranean through the dirty windows of the train.

# LOSING CONTROL

AS JÉROME'S BODY was washed down the river in the direction of the sea and Thomas drove towards Vintimiglia, Josef Havel looked at Amra over the table of the Palme d'Or restaurant in the Martinez Hôtel. What he saw pleased him beyond measure. He had to admit he had always been a breast man and Amra's firm generous bosom seemed to beckon him and promise untold pleasure.

With a view over the Croisette and the sea, waiters prancing obsequiously around them, everything had gone perfectly. The day after their first meeting, she had agreed to an early lunch with him. Smoked salmon with champagne, followed by "médaillon de veau" and a bottle of Domaine d'Ott. He was totally infatuated. That pink mouth – God, how she licked her lips! Should he try to get her back for coffee? Was it too early?

Amra continued to play her part. She was making it easy for him but not too easy. She didn't want to disturb him, make him suspicious in any way. She knew he wouldn't be able to resist taking her back to his apartment. She thought about Faruk's gun in her bag. She thought about the grenade. She thought about the first shot in the stomach. Then one bullet in each knee and one in each arm. One in the groin. Tape across the helpless, screaming man's mouth. The grenade, with its release attached to one end of a length of string.

She smiled sweetly up at Havel's face. He felt his body quivering, his heart beating fast and the pressure building in his veins. The moment had come to ask her back. He took a generous sip of wine, poured both her and himself another glass and breathed in. Before he could say a word, his mobile rang. It was Thomas.

Amra tried not to show her disappointment when Josef told her he had to leave on urgent business. He tried not to show how he no longer felt on top of the situation. His heart was beating wildly with frustration.

%

Thomas had called him as soon as he reached Monaco. He said simply that something serious had gone wrong and that he would have to talk about it face to face. They agreed to meet at Josef's apartment on the Cap d'Antibes. Thomas collected his car, drove up to the motorway tunnel above Eze, threw his parking ticket out of the window and headed towards Antibes at a leisurely pace, stopping off at his flat to leave the rucksack.

He ruminated about Josef's state of mind at that moment. He could imagine him scowling, furious, trying to work out what might have gone wrong. Thomas was going to make it realistic, the whole story, implicitly it would be his fault and this was why Josef would believe him.

Havel stamped about his apartment like a wounded bear. What the hell had happened? Surely the money hadn't gone? What if the police had stopped Jérôme? He thought about the girl and swore again. Instead of screwing her and drinking champagne . . . no, no, he meant instead of making love to her and drinking champagne . . . he stopped still, momentarily shocked by his pious reflection. Was this really him talking to himself like this? Was it possible that he, Vuk Racik, was not even allowing himself the right to speak irreverently about a woman inside his own head?

The humour of the situation suddenly hit him. It was fucking funny when he thought about it. Vuk, the toughest bastard in town, simpering like a love-struck adolescent.

He poured himself a drink, lit a cigarette and stared into the big mirror above the fireplace, blowing smoke into his reflection. Must be getting soft, he thought. A few months ago, he'd been fighting a bloody war, for God's sake, risking his life every day, killing people (he corrected himself – not people – Bosnian Muslims, the filthy swine who wanted to steal the land belonging to the Serbs, the mad Mullahs who preached death to those who didn't believe in Allah).

He had dominated and controlled his dangerous, over-ambitious colleagues, he had channelled weapons supplied from Eastern Europe off to Libya, Chad and Afghanistan, getting paid in cash. He had personally confronted Milosovic about a strategy disagreement. Now he was uptight because he'd have to wait a couple of days before screwing a bit of Spanish pussy.

He laughed out loud and continued drinking and was in a far better mood than Thomas expected when he arrived 20 minutes later.

"OK, Thomas. Give it to me. What's all this shit about? What the fuck's gone wrong? I can't believe anything that serious has happened. Nothing we can't sort out."

Thomas helped himself to a drink, which was unusual for him, braced himself and looked Josef in the eyes.

"That Jérôme bastard. He didn't stop off at fucking Monaco this time. He just drove on. All the way to Italy. I followed, of course, no problem, but he crossed the border two cars ahead of me. He couldn't have known I was following. I don't think so, anyway. There was a delay. The customs officers checked out the car in front of me. Two minutes, that was all, but enough for me to lose Jérôme. I saw him turn towards Vintimiglia instead of taking the motorway towards Milan but the trouble is after that there is a T-junction, you either go towards Turin or you go towards the centre of town. I took the chance of going into Vintimiglia and drove around. Then I saw his fucking car parked in front of the train station. I waited for an hour, first checking out the trains and the platforms.

"There was a train that left for Rome 10 minutes earlier, and another that was going the other way to Marseilles which left one minute after the other one. Both trains had multiple stops. If he got either of those trains he could have got off anywhere. That's why I didn't drive to Rome straight away. I needed to talk to you. We've got to speak to that bastard of a bank manager. The cunt must know about this, he must know where his fucking assistant is, what the hell….."

Havel went pale. He got hold of a large leather armchair, lifted it like a cushion and hurled it against the wall.

"Thomas, you're not supposed to make mistakes like that. If I ask you to follow someone, you stick to his fucking arse, you keep so close you can smell the hair on the back of his neck . . ."

Thomas cut in "You didn't want him to know he was being followed. I kept as close as possible. The customs delay was just bad luck. Do you know how much he had with him?"

Thomas thought about the four million dollars he had discovered upon opening the rucksack in his flat.

Josef stared at the upturned armchair and narrowed his eyes. "He normally took a million at a time. That's why everything's taken so long. If he's done a runner would he have run with just a million? He must have taken more. I'm going to go and see that stupid arsehole, Lucas. But I'll wait until tomorrow afternoon, just to be sure Jérôme really has disappeared. You never know, he may have had car problems and continued by train…….."

Thomas frowned. Something could still go wrong.

# REALLY WORRIED

%

LUCAS HAD SET UP A BEER. Jérôme was always so punctual. It was exactly 12.25h. He had ordered Afligen, a strong hoppy Belgian beer. He drank his own and ordered another. At 12.40h he drank Jérôme's beer then he called Jérôme's mobile number and left a message.

"Where the fuck are you, you lazy French git? If you want your beer, you'd better get your arse over here, quick. Call me as soon as you get the message."

By 13.15, Lucas was seriously worried. His hands had started sweating, always a bad sign and a familiar alcoholic cloud had settled in his head, dulling his panic but dulling his mind even more. When he staggered back into the bank, the staff looked at him politely but with visible embarrassment.

Solange walked up to him. "Mr Watt, would you like a coffee?"

Lucas slurred. "Why, do I look as if I need one?"

Solange laughed cheerfully. "Not at all, Sir, but you usually have one after lunch. I'll bring it into your office. By the way, you'll have to tell me where I can find Jérôme. His clients all seem to be calling with urgent requests that I can't handle. I'll be with you in a second."

Lucas walked unsteadily through to the washroom, urinated, washed his hands and splashed cold water on his face. He looked at himself in the mirror. Bad. It wasn't the alcohol so much as the rictus of worry and tension which he couldn't hide, even when he tried feebly to force a smile at himself.

He went back to the office, where Solange was waiting. "Solange, I'm afraid we may have to wait a bit. Jérôme told me he was seeing very important clients in Italy today and he would have to keep his mobile off most of the time. All we can do is hang around until he calls."

Solange frowned. "I don't understand, Mr Watt. I had him on the mobile yesterday. He told me he was having lunch with you today and then coming back to the office. He said he would be in jeans because he was having a half day off and he wouldn't be able to change into his suit before coming back to the bank. I don't . . . I don't understand."

Lucas snapped at her. "Solange, stop saying you don't understand.You're not here to understand. Just do as you're told. If Jérôme changes his plans, it's his business, not yours. If there are urgent phone calls, put them through to me."

Solange froze in surprise. Lucas never spoke to her in this fashion. Then she ran out of his office, crying. Lucas cursed his ineptitude and drank his coffee. It was a full hour before he had his first JB.

Three hours later, his mobile phone rang. He jumped at it, knocking over his freshly poured drink. It was Isabelle, Jérôme's wife.

"Hi, Lucas. Sorry to bother you. I've been trying to get Jérôme but his mobile doesn't seem to be working and he's not in the office. Any ideas?"

This was the call Lucas had been dreading. Any ideas? He had too many bloody ideas. That was the whole problem. There was no way Jérôme would have scarpered with the money. Something terrible had happened, he was sure of it.

"Oh, hi, Isabelle – don't worry about that silly husband of yours – you know what he's like. He's always doing disappearing tricks. I do know he had to go to Italy this afternoon, unexpectedly. It may be a while before he calls."

Lucas put the phone down, picked up his glass which had not broken on the carpeted floor and stared at the ceiling. He bit his lip, hesitated a second and then went over to the drinks trolley again.

Out of habit and to focus his mind away from the crisis he picked up his brochure about alcoholism and read on with masochistic resignation:

ALCOHOLISM CAN KILL

People with advanced alcoholism drink almost constantly; have trouble keeping a job; relate poorly to others; and may have self-destructive impulses, including frequent thoughts of suicide. Some of the serious physical consequences of late-stage alcoholism are convulsions, hallucinations, mental confusion, partial paralysis, and/or cirrhosis of the liver. The longer alcoholism goes without treatment, the greater the damage to the body. Untreated alcoholism is potentially fatal.

The way things were going Lucas was indeed beginning to fear a fatal conclusion and he hadn't even spoken to Havel yet. He wandered round his office and reflected on whether or not he should just go on drinking until he passed out. As he got more drunk, he wished he were somewhere else, someone else, even that he didn't exist at all.

But somewhere at the back of his mind a tiny light still flickered, signaling to him that if only he could take a grip and stop drinking the situation was still manageable and not as hideously worrying as his whisky soaked brain and emotions were informing him.

%

It was already 17.30h. Josef called Lucas' office number. Lucas was still reeling from the second call he had just finished with Isabelle. Jérôme's wife had been calm but there was a definite undercurrent of anxiety. He had told her not to worry, of course, that the mobile was switched off because he was with clients, but she hadn't seemed totally reassured. He had told her again to call back if she had any news.

Havel's voice terrified him. "Lucas, you'd better have a fucking good explanation."

Lucas kept his voice calm as his stomach churned. "Listen, Josef, I suppose you're talking about Jérôme. Well, he's not that late and if it gets much later I'm going to look for him myself. I'll call you back and we'll see each other tomorrow morning. You have absolutely nothing to worry about." His voice began to slur.

"You'd better be absolutely right, Lucas, that there's absolutely nothing to worry about because, if you're wrong, you're the one that's going to be more worried than anyone else. Any missing money and you repay it personally – just remember that you drunken lout."

Lucas slumped back into his armchair, feeling so shattered that he couldn't even raise his glass to his lips.

# SECOND VISIT

WHILE EVENTS CONNECTING JOSEF, Lucas, Amra, Thomas and Jérôme had, or were in the process of building up to a crescendo, George, involved, but ignorant of many of the gory details, decided to take another morning off from "Le Yacht" and spend it with his friend. Two days had now gone by since his first visit with Amra to Faruk's bedside and the patient was making significant progress.

He was obviously in great pain but only accepted morphine in the evening before going to sleep for the night. The pain during the day kindled his hatred and helped focus his mind. He could talk, see, move his arms and head. His lower limbs remained immobilised. Amra came to see him every day and had agreed to relay with George.

"So how is she?" Faruk asked.

"Aren't we supposed to be asking you that question?" replied George with raised eyebrows.

"You can see for yourselves, I'm totally fucked but happy and satisfied, like the daughter of the commanding officer of the barracks." This somewhat cumbersome formula was a standing joke between the two and George was elated to see his friend employ it. The road to recovery.

"Now, tell me about Amra. I'm worried about her."

George thought for a few seconds, unsure."Well, she's fine I guess, burning with energy. She's totally consumed with her plans for Vuk Racik. She's told you how it's all panning out I guess? "

"Yeah, she's told me but I'm not sure I believe her. She says Saleh and his mates are going to corner him when he returns to the apartment on the Cap d'Antibes. She says they're going to throw my hand grenade at him, close enough to blast him off his feet but not close enough to kill him, and then finish him off with bullets which will be administered one by one so he dies in agony."

George winced and wiped the back of his hand across his forehead.

"They've got my revolver and a couple of shotguns. If that lot doesn't finish him off nothing will. I don't know, I feel she's hiding something. I can't believe she's going to delegate this thing to Saleh. She's going to want to be there, maybe even try and do it on her own, be the one who pulls the trigger.

"Trouble is Saleh swears to me it's true. George, if you can find out something please let me know. Don't fool me please, I'm already incapacitated, there is nothing worse than not being certain about what is going on. I'm worried and I'm stuck in this fucking bed. Paralysed George, fucking paralysed. I should be the one executing the bastard. If my sister tries she'll probably get blown away herself."

George reflected upon all of this. It was true, Amra was behaving strangely, which he'd thought understandable given the circumstances but she was out of character, there was a lie somewhere. He was sure she was hiding something.

"I will investigate as well as I can. Don't worry though, if anyone can look after herself it's Amra."

"O.K. thanks George, now can I ask you something else? I need stimulation, provocation. Ask me questions, make me think. I need to get my brain into gear, I'm in a fog, I feel as if I've been drugged." Faruk moved his torso slightly, frowned with frustration again.

"You are drugged for God's sake! The nurse told me she gives you a fair old shot of morphine in the evening. She can't believe you refuse it during the day. Your ribs man! You were literally punctured by the handle bars of the motorbike. Christ knows how you survived. It's weird when you think about it. Both of us having motorbike accidents. Yours was worse of course."

Faruk was silent again , for a moment, and then he spoke, making a feeble click of his fingers. "I know what we're going to talk about: religion!"

George couldn't suppress a chuckle. "Religion? Come on man, that's a bit morbid isn't it, with you lying in a hospital bed."

Faruk shook his head. " Not at all. I'll tell why I thought about it. It's just that I would never blaspheme like you."

"Like what?" George was now intrigued.

"Like when you say 'Christ knows this and for God's sake that.'"

George laughed scornfully. "That's not blasphemy, it's just a manner of speaking. I don't even believe in God to tell you the truth. Jesus existed and all that, but he was conceived like you and me, in a hot passionate moment of lust and love with the usual exchange of bodily fluids. Might have been an immaculate fuck but certainly not an immaculate conception."

For the first time Faruk laughed, although his laugh turned into a croak as he creased with pain.

"You really are an infidel George. Do you have any idea how offended a Christian believer would be if he heard what you just said?"

"Yes, I suppose so but that's what pisses me off in a way. They believe one thing, I believe another thing but I'm the only one who has to be careful about what he says. I mean they invent all the mumbo jumbo to get a ticket to heaven and immortality and

I'm supposed to humour them and all their pious bullshit while they tell me I'm destined to go to hell." George sighed. " Actually I couldn't give a stuff."

"You must be a bit miserable George , underneath that cheerful exterior. How can you live with the idea that when you die that's it? What's the point? The clock is ticking away, even while you're talking to me, and you're closer every second to disappearing, definitively, off the face of the earth. Thanks, incidentally, for investing so much of the precious and limited time you have left talking to me. Seriously, how do you do it?"

George looked slightly perplexed and then regained his composure.

"I'll give you my brother's response to that question: spirits not spirituality. Drink enough JB and you can cope. Mankind needs a tranquiliser Faruk, I guess my brother and I go for booze and you go for God. Different ways of facing up to the inevitable, coping with angst, the human condition. You asked me to provoke you. OK, well if you want the truth I think religion is a dead bore, it's off the peg spirituality holding out the promise of the eternal if you conform to the wishes of the mad mullahs and the pompous priests. It's a fairy tale with a dose of mysticism to explain the unexplainable and control the masses. It's..."

Faruk cut in, with a mixture of scorn and pity. "That is so feeble George. You want to reduce everything to a few cynical phrases; it's empty rhetoric George, it's not really you talking. No one disbelieves totally. You're deeper than that. You know you can't dismiss Mohamed, Jesus, Buddha, Confucius........."

"Excuse me, my turn to cut in" interrupted George. "Listen to what I'm saying. They may all be great men with great spiritual thoughts and an example to all of us. But I don't have to go to church or believe in God or Allah to know I shouldn't kill or steal or covet other blokes' wives (mind you, not much one can do about that). Do you know what the greatest book in the world is?"

"The Bible, the Karma Sutra, I don't know."

"Wrong again my friend. It's *The Brothers Karamazov* . Dostoevsky. Read that while you've got time on your hands and you're stuck in this dump. You'll see what I mean. It's not just a great detective story but a great spiritual quest. And guess what? I've bought it for you."

George handed over two volumes to Faruk. On top was a deliberately absurd Get Well Soon card with a picture of a patient covered from head to foot in plaster, staring with bulging eyes at his nurse's breasts as she puts a spoonful of bromide in his tea.

Faruk was slightly overwhelmed. He was not used to receiving presents and the gesture left him momentarily speechless.

"You are my brother George."

Faruk quickly wiped away a tear which George pretended not to notice and, with superb and uniquely English skill, airily appearing to be unaware of the emotion in the room replied with cheerful neutrality: "Suits me mate, always wanted a brother about my age. Fed up with that old fart Lucas."

There was a moment's silence while Faruk rested. Then he opened his eyes again."Do you want me to tell you my version of God?"

George disliked this sort of intimacy. It was alright changing in front of total strangers in the locker room before a game of rugby but other people talking about their faith embarrassed him. Still, anything Faruk wanted.

"Go for it. Enlighten me," he said with gentle irony.

"O.K." Faruk concentrated as he gathered his thoughts. Then he fell profoundly asleep.

# LIES DAMNED LIES

THE NEXT MORNING LUCAS took the lift up to the bank and reflected on how weak he felt. His vital strength seemed to have drained away. In Chloé's arms the previous night and after a few whiskies he had felt temporarily calm. But in the morning, after a bad night's sleep and facing reality again, he felt drained and depressed. It was as if his whole life was in question, not just because of the immediate danger. What was he doing? Why, how had he steered himself into this murky, sordid situation? Was it the simple and inevitable culmination of years of complacency and greed?

He still managed to look cheerful when he entered the bank and greeted his staff normally (although he was aware of their growing concern) but rapidly sought shelter in the haven of his office, closed the door and began ruminating. It was 9am. Josef Havel - who the fuck was he? – would be arriving at 9.45am. He had a little time to collect his thoughts. But his sense of panic quickly took over and he had no idea what he was going to say.

He would tell him that he had warned him that it was a risky business. He would tell him he had never given any guarantees. He would tell him it was impossible to continue the business. Havel would have to find someone else. What he had in Liechtenstein was safe. Jérôme's disappearance was . . . . . .

Havel came into his office without knocking. He sat down opposite Lucas and stared at him in silence. Then he quietly put a revolver on the desk.

"So where the fuck is my money, Lucas? Where the fuck is your side-kick? What the fuck is going on? I want my money back, Lucas, or you might just as well jump off the top of the Negresco".

Lucas stared first at the enormous man in front of him and then at the revolver. He couldn't help a nervous laugh. The situation was so wildly out of control now that there was nothing he could do to save it. But to his astonishment, his mind suddenly started functioning and his fear ebbed away. Everything was so bizarre, so like a bad film . . . so like a game. So play it as if it were a game.

"Josef, think a bit. What are you threatening me for? Just because my side-kick, as you call him, is no longer around doesn't mean you lost any money. I've phoned the bank in Vaduz." Lucas lied smoothly, he'd been doing that all his career he reflected.

"There was a $200.000 deposit made on the company account the same day Jérôme disappeared, i.e. yesterday, but late, well after normal bank hours and after we spoke on the telephone. There is no way anyone else could have made it except our account signatory and he only does it when Jerome delivers the money. So that means he took the money in, made the usual arrangements. You get my meaning? Jérôme didn't just disappear. He's been kidnapped or murdered, but after depositing the money. Probably by somebody who knew what he was doing. So who knew about what he was doing apart from you and me, Josef?"

Havel was temporarily taken aback my Lucas' counter-attack. Then his eyes narrowed, and he said "My God." Then he fell into silence again. Thomas? He tried to recover the advantage. "You tell me, Lucas, who else knew? There's nobody my side."

"Then why did you say 'My God'? Come on, Josef. There's no point in pretending you can't think of someone. What about your side-kick? I assume he's your side-kick. The guy who drops you off occasionally at the tennis courts. Does he know anything? Could he have followed Jérôme and killed him, hoping he'd got the money? Tell me."

"Fuck you, Lucas." Havel stood up and put the revolver back in his pocket.

"I'm going to think about this." Havel strode out.

Lucas felt the relief spread through his body. He'd managed to rattle the bastard, fend him off for a while. Then he realised that if he had touched on the truth while improvising with him, it meant that Jérome was dead for sure. And that made him want to cry. A fresh surge of panic hit him like a train as he contemplated his own likely fate. He started trembling.

The securities clerk poked his head politely round the door.

"Goodbye Monsieur, I'm off on holiday. I've got to go now and pick up the wife and kids. And the mother in law! If I don't come back you'll know I'm in prison for murdering her. No, it'll be OK. She's not that bad. Anyway, thanks for allowing me the week off and see you soon. We're going to Perpignan."

Lucas nodded and gave what was intended to look like a cheery wave. Oh for normality. He'd change places with the man without hesitation. He imagined him for a moment driving his second hand Peugeot station-wagon, plump wife by his side, mother in law clucking in the back with the well-behaved children. He pictured the crammed boot, the roof-rack, the unity. That was what life was all about, not his hedonistic individualism, his constant scramble for money, his anaesthetising drinks.

Too bad. He gritted his teeth and concentrated on quelling the anguish in his stomach and the tears which were again filling his eyes.

# RECOVERY

THE SHOCK OF THE COLD WATER, which cascaded down from the snow-capped mountains behind the Col de Tende, hit Jérôme like a thousand volts. His stumble at the edge of the river had led to Thomas' normally deadly accurate shots missing his heart by millimetres. One bullet had smashed a rib and exited just below his sternum. The other was lodged in the space between his heart and lungs. After a few minutes he passed out again, his left foot caught in a branch overhanging the river and his head just above the water, resting on a small boulder. Occasionally, a change in the current or an eddy would send a ripple of water over the boulder, causing his head to sway and loll, like a broken doll's.

He regained consciousness ten minutes later. His mind had gone blank, he couldn't remember what had happened. All he knew was that he was dying. He tried to move and failed. It hurt too much. But the deep chill in his whole body hurt more than his ripped flesh and splintered rib. Panic seized him and tears started flowing down his cheeks. He prayed to God to save him. He saw a kind, wise face looking down at him. You can do it. Pull, push, come on. Your legs are working. Get your foot away from the branch. Hold on to the rocks at the side. They're covered with slimy moss. They're slippery. Fuck you Jérome, No excuses.

He gave one last kick and rolled out of the water onto the rock-strewn bank. The afternoon sunshine slowly warmed his body and dried his clothes. Enough to help him survive the night despite his loss of blood, before he was found the following morning by a hiker, Vitorio Tomba.

Vitorio hated trouble and he hated anything that reminded him of death. At first his instinct told him to avoid the body and pretend that he hadn't seen it. But there was a tiny, subcutaneous glow behind the terrifying pallor of the man's face. Something in the body's position which signalled life, a residual vital tautness which denied both the initial slackness of death and its subsequent frozen immobility.

He scrambled up the road and waved down a car. Within an hour, Jérôme was in Vintimiglia hospital. Within another hour he had the bullet removed. The police officer sent to watch over him waited patiently as the exhausted man slept. He felt drowsy himself as he counted the little bubbles from the drip-feed.

Occasionally Jérôme twitched and quivered. Like a dog dreaming of rabbits thought the policeman. Who was he? He had no papers on him and he couldn't even guess his nationality. Mediterranean extraction, no doubt about it . What had he done to be shot and thrown into a river? He stood up, stretched and went to get another cup of coffee from the machine in the corridor.

# GEORGE SUMS UP

JÉRÔME SLEPT. His wife fretted and wept. Havel moped about Amparo who hadn't returned his call. Thomas recounted his money.

It was early evening and Lucas slumped back, as usual, with an enormous JB while Chloé pottered about in the kitchen, looking worried. George observed his brother and suddenly smiled in a tight lipped fashion.

"Lucas, I don't know what's bugging you but you look like something the cat's brought in. You know, sometimes I wonder why I even bothered coming down to the Côte d'Azur. This place is crazy. There seems to be nothing but mayhem in this part of the world. I would have been better off in my poky little dump in London.

" Sorry, but you could make a film out of this. Let me just sum things up : within a few weeks, you've turned into a soak, you're involved in dicey fucking business with some Czech second-hand car salesman called Havel (which, incidentally, seems to be going drastically wrong – I assume that's what's bugging you) , Amra's brother gets knocked off his bike and may end up ...."

George looked at Amra who was staring out of the window and apologised.

"......there seems to be a diabolical manhunt going on for a mass murderer called Vuk Racik, in turn orchestrated by Bosnian refugees, and now Jérôme has disappeared. Am I just imagining all of this or is that a fair summary?"

There was silence for a moment. George and Lucas looked at Amra again. She was staring into the middle distance with her hand raised as if she was holding a wand.

"What second-hand car salesman?" She asked. Her voice was so quiet the two men had to lean forward to hear her.

George replied, "I never told you about him, Amra. Don't worry, it's got nothing to do with anyone except my stupid brother here, who won't admit it but is, in my opinion, heavily in the shit with this eastern European bloke. Can't really talk about it, can we, Lucas? Wouldn't be respecting client confidentiality, would it? Matter of principle, isn't that right, Lucas?"

"Oh, go and take a flying fuck at a rolling doughnut, will you? I don't need sarcasm now. I just don't need it. If you want to help, just shut it."

George grimaced and stood up to fetch the JB. He made to pour out a glass of white wine for Amra but stopped as she put her hand over her glass.

"Strange name," she said. "Did you say Havel?" George nodded.

Amra almost laughed. This was too much. Surely to God Lucas couldn't be involved with Vuk Racik? She suddenly understood that her supposedly marginal role in events surrounding Lucas and his brother might have become a crucial one. It was as if she was now responsible for everybody's fate. She would kill Vuk Racik whatever happened. But what was the fallout from all of this? Would it be positive or negative for George and Lucas? They sounded more than worried, and with Lucas being a bank manager there had to be money involved, and if it came from Racik it had to be dirty money. Of course! Dicey business was what George had said. Cash. It had to be cash.

Bit by bit the evening dragged on and Amra became more and more silent. Lucas and George were both drunk and Chloé was asleep, curled up in an armchair. Amra stood up, gave Lucas and George a kiss and went to bed. She heard the trickle of conversation through her bedroom door, on and off as she tried to focus her mind. After a couple of hours she went to sleep.

When she woke up Lucas had already left the flat and Chloé was still sleeping. There was the smell of stale tobacco and spirits in the living room and kitchen.

Amra stared out of the window, seeking a solution. Then she opened all the windows and swept up the debris.

If she told George about this sinister and barely credible coincidence, he might alert the police and she would never get her revenge. If she didn't tell him, Lucas might be in greater danger than he imagined. In fact, he almost certainly was. George was the problem. There was something naive about him, a lack of cunning. George belonged to a more innocent world.

She decided to tell Lucas herself. If he then told George, that was up to him. But she would discourage him. Lucas must have suspected that there was more to Havel than met the eye. But what would he do if he discovered that Havel was Vuk and that Vuk was a mass murderer? She couldn't help a small giggle as she imagined George including this fact in his summary of events the previous evening.

She looked at her watch. It was 9.30h. George was still asleep. He had talked and drunk with Lucas until the small hours of the morning. Christ, Lucas must be feeling bad. He wouldn't feel better when he heard what she had to say. She picked up the telephone and called the bank. Lucas seemed irritated and distant but agreed to meet her at 10.00h.

# THE TRUTH

BY 10.30h THE SAME MORNING, Jérôme came round. He felt as if he had been gutted like a fish, lying on his back in a strange world of white linen, chrome and glass. He saw the nurse and the policeman chatting quietly in the corner of his room and closed his eyes again. He went over events in his mind, and as his memory flooded back he opened his eyes again, suddenly horribly aware of the full significance of everything that had happened. He tried to call the policeman over but his throat was too dry. He lifted his hand, noted the drip-feed leading into his vein and attracted attention.

Both persons bent over him, the nurse holding his wrist to take his pulse, talking quietly to him in Italian. The policeman said nothing, looking down with calm detachment.

"I need a phone," croaked Jérôme. "A phone, please." The nurse gave him some water.

The policeman replied, also in Italian, "Keep calm. You're OK. You need to rest and then answer some questions. We'll bring you a phone. What's your name and who do you want to call?"

"I have to call my wife. She must be going crazy. She'll have alerted half of France by now. My name's Jérôme."

The nurse wheeled over a tray designed to overhang the patient's bed and placed the standard ward telephone on it.

"Can I be on my own, please?" There were tears in Jérôme's eyes as he thought of what he was going to say to Isabelle. The nurse nodded and indicated to the policeman to leave the room with her.

"Five minutes, Mr Jérôme. Then you must rest and take your medicine. Jérôme nodded, waited for the door to close and then decided to dial Lucas' mobile.

"Jérôme, Jérôme, for Christ's sake, I'd given up on you. What . . . what?" Lucas clutched the side of his desk and sat up straight, then stood.

"Listen, Lucas, I'm OK. Listen and I'll give you the bare details. These guys are murderers, Lucas. The side-kick, Thomas, or whatever his name is, thinks I'm dead. He shot me, for fuck's sake, shot me and left me to drown in a fucking river. I'm OK, I'm in hospital in Vintimiglia. Lucas, what do we do? We're shafted, whatever happens. I'd rather stay alive. Call the police, Lucas. We'll end up in jail too, but that's better than being bumped off by those bastards. Do it, Lucas. Unless you've got a private jet somewhere and we can fly to Cost Rica right now."

Lucas stared into the receiver as if it was some reptile about to bite his nose off.

"Jérôme, this is crazy. Oh Jesus am I happy to hear the sound of your voice, but.....shit man. This morning, you've no idea what's been going on. Isabelle has already alerted the police, who told her to piss off because you're not considered to be missing unless you've been gone for more than 48 hours. I've had Josef here already – he thinks you've stolen the cash but I told him I'd had confirmation it was already in the bank. And, Amra's just been here. That was bad news. And, you know what she told me? You know where the bastard comes from? Yugoslavia man, Yugoslavia. He's one of those Serb warlords, for God's sake. This is money from arms, drugs, prostitution, theft, you name it. Jesus, you can imagine internal audit getting hold of this. They'd shit in their fucking pants, man. Which, incidentally, is what I'm doing right now. Jérôme, listen, I think I've got to run for it. There's still 9 million dollars in the safe."

Jérôme gasped. "Wait a second. You've just made me think: of course – 9 million dollars! Lucas , listen, for God's sake! You've got to get a car now, you've got to get a fucking Espace, lots of room, load the cash in and then you've got to pick up Chloé, you've got to pick up George and you've got to pick up Isabelle and the kids. Then you just start driving. Anyone I've forgotten?"

"What about your goldfish?"

Jérôme winced. Laughing was impossible. If he hadn't been on a strong painkiller mixed into the drip-feed he wouldn't have been able to speak.

"No, seriously," Lucas continued, "I'll have to get that Amra girl too. Mind you, it might be an idea to leave her behind 'cos she said she was going to knock off Havel. His name's Vuk Racik, by the way."

Jérôme considered things for a minute. What a mess.

"Listen, forget Isabelle and the kids. I'll tell them myself and get them to come over here independently. You can't round up everyone. You look after your lot. Just one other thing. What about dividing the enemy? What about sowing the seeds of their mutual destruction? What about telling Racik now about what has happened? Get him off your back for a while."

Lucas slapped his forehead. "Of course! Of course! You know, I already told Havel, Racik, whatever his sodding name is, that Thomas might have a hand in your disappearance. But I was inventing it. I never thought it might be true. They seemed too close to start ripping each other off."

Jérôme interrupted him. "Call Havel, Racik, I mean, and tell him to go to Thomas' apartment. Tell him to check it out for hidden goodies. There's 4 million dollars for fuck's sake. That will take time and give him the proof. Then he's going to be so mad he's going to forget his bank manager and go and slit Thomas' throat. With a bit of luck, they might finish each other off. Whatever happens, it will give you enough time to round up your sheep and get away to Italy. Then we get back in touch. Keep your mobile on whatever you do."

Lucas had momentarily forgotten his fear. The possibility, however slim, of saving the situation charged him up immediately. He was almost having fun.

"I've got to think a bit more clearly. First – why Italy? Why not Corsica? Chloé's mother lives there. Way down in Porto Vecchio, off the beaten track. She's always begging us to go down there. I've never been, in case she thought it meant I was going to get married. Man, if she can hide us there for a while, I'll marry Chloé twice over – I'll invite the Queen of England, I'll wear a pink tuxedo, I'll...... That's where we're going, Jérôme. No frontiers. Corsica is France. No baggage being checked, get it? And Racik is going to automatically think we've gone abroad."

"Good thinking, Lucas."

They said goodbye. Jérôme slumped back on his pillow exhausted, unable for 10 minutes even to call Isabelle. He panted quietly.

Lucas stared into the middle distance. Good thinking, yes. But was he capable of turning his thoughts into action?

He tried to focus clearly. No sleep, weeks of alcohol. Weeks of gross consumption, years of heavy consumption. He picked up the brochure and crumpled it in his hand and threw it violently into the wastepaper basket. Time to take a grip.

Objective? Get the hell out of Nice with $9,000,000 and live happily ever after. Constraints? One big mother fucker of a Serbian murderer who was going to try and get him sooner or later. Sooner, in fact. Other priorities? Get Chloé and George. Get taxis. Constraints? Phone Vuk, get him on the trail of Thomas. Bank? Tell Solange that Jérôme was now reachable on the mobile to quell any suspicions and tell her he, Lucas, had to go to Zurich to meet an important client – get her to book a ticket – yes!

"Solange, this is a crazy morning," he said into the telephone. "I've had Jérôme on the line, he's back but in bed with flu or something.....or somebody if you ask me. Getting his end away eh? Give him a few days, is what I say and then I'll fire him. Ha, ha!"

Solange listened to Lucas as neutrally as possible and wondered if he was drunk again.

" Anyway, that's one story," Lucas continued in an excitable fashion. "The other thing is, guess who called me? My number one prospect, Hans Kaliken. He wants to meet me in Zurich and for me to take all those documents we've been holding in the safe for him. Get me a 1$^{st}$ class ticket with Swiss Air, there's a flight at 12.45h. I'll just have time to go home and get a clean shirt. Have the ticket waiting for me at the airport. Oh, and if anyone calls, you can tell them where I am, that's not a problem, and that I'll be back tomorrow evening on the 18.30 flight. Thanks, Solange."

Lucas phoned Corsica Ferries and booked two cabins. The ferry was leaving at 13.15h. He would have to move fast. It was already 11.00h. Racik would have already seen Thomas and doubtless been convinced that the latter had nothing to do with Jérome's disappearance. He would be back, firing on all cylinders. He picked up his telephone and called, pitching his voice at what he thought was the right level to communicate indignation and firmness.

"Josef, listen. This is important. You're not going to like it,I bullshitted you this morning about the money having been deposited in Vaduz. I was scared. You know that. I had no fucking clue where Jérôme was. I needed time to think."

Vuk interrupted him. "You bet I don't like this. You can also bet that I'm going to kick your arse and cut your miserable little faggot's bollocks off. Where's the money, Lucas? You've got five seconds to reply."

Lucas felt the old panic mounting inside him again, gritted his teeth and replied. "If you want an answer, if you want the truth, you'd do better listening to me instead of hurling insults and threats at me. I'm going to tell you where the money is . . . where I think it is."

Vuk roared over the telephone again. "Not where you think it is. I'm not interested in what you think, you cunt, I want facts . . ."

Lucas worked himself up into a histrionic rage, not without a genuine grain of desperate fury.

"Shut your fucking mouth and open your fucking ears, because this is the last time I'm going to be interrupted. Guess who called this morning, Josef. Guess. You don't know, do you? Well, it was Jérôme who's in a sodding hospital in Milan with two sodding great bullet holes.

"And guess who put the bullets in him, Josef. Want to know? Your little side-kick, Thomas, or whatever his stupid name is. So if you want the money you'd better go and interview the bastard, and I'm sure you'll know how to persuade him to give you the truth. Just do what I say, Josef. Be rational, do what I say. I'm telling you. I'm on the mobile, you can call me any minute of the day or night. But just get one thing straight. Thomas is the man you need to see. Not me, and certainly not Jérôme, who should be dead. Over and out, Josef."

Lucas pushed the red button on his mobile and sat back sweating but, weirdly, enjoying himself. His self-respect had just shot up a few hundred percent. He glanced at the bottle of JB and refused. Then he allowed himself one small gulp, directly out of the bottle and lit a cigarette, his mind wandering furiously. Passport, suitcases, George, Chloé . . .

# SURPRISE

VUK SMILED TO HIMSELF. This was beginning to be interesting. Far better to know, if it was true, that there was a traitor in the camp. He'd have to be careful with Thomas, he was dangerous. Very dangerous. But not as dangerous as him. And he had the advantage of surprise. He had scheduled a meeting with Thomas at 11.30h in Antibes, in his apartment. He would not cancel but drive over to Nice and break into Thomas' flat while he wasn't there. If he found the money, that was it. If he didn't, that left the possibility that Lucas was bullshitting. In which case, things were really messy and he was going to have to start thinking from scratch.

Then he realised that whatever happened, whether Lucas was telling the truth or not, he would have to get rid of him too, and put a third bullet into Jérôme.

They knew too much now. They'd check out his identity and he'd never be 100% secure.What if they took their commission and then put the C.I.A. or MI6 onto his trail? Vuk patted the new hunting knife he had strapped to his calf and checked his revolver. Then he set off from his flat to Nice. He knew Thomas always took the "*bord de mer*" road so he stuck to the "National 7" and reached the urban highway which crossed the town of Nice by 11.25h. Within 5 minutes he had exited at "St Philippe", driven down Boulevard Grosso and turned left into a street next to Avenue des Fleurs.

He entered Thomas' building and walked up to the second floor instead of taking the lift. His mobile rang. It was Thomas. He froze and listened.

"Are you there, Vuk? I'm outside your place ringing the bell."

"Stay there, Thomas. I'll be back in 15 minutes. Got tied up. Get yourself a coffee in the bar down the road. I'll call you back if there's any further delay."

Perfect. He hung up. Now he knew he was completely safe. He walked up to Thomas' door and tested it. It was obviously double-locked, it didn't budge a millimetre. He walked up and down the small corridor, putting his ear next to the three other doors which corresponded to Thomas' neighbours. There was no sound, no talking, no clatter of dishes being washed, or television sets or music.

He screwed on the silencer of his revolver and, barely making a sound, shot a clean hole through both of the locks. The door just needed one violent kick and it swung open. The flat was sparsely furnished and neat. Vuk walked over to the wardrobe and carefully went through the shelves and drawers. He checked the top and tapped the floor. He heaved up one side and crouched to look underneath. Nothing.

He was just going to check the bathroom and toilet reservoir when, tilting his head back, he noticed there was a neat, barely discernible crack around one of the panels which had been used to create a false ceiling. He pulled over a chair and pushed the panel. It lifted easily and he patted and groped around the inside. His hand immediately touched the rucksack. He pulled it down and stared in silence. He'd never quite been able to believe that Thomas was capable of this. His hands trembled with anger as he picked it up and walked back down to his car.

He called Thomas again. His voice was the same as always. Deep and authoritative. "Thomas, sorry, I think we're going to have to change our plans. I've just had the bank manager on the line. His nerves are getting out of control. He wants to take everything that's left in the safe in Nice over to Liechtenstein now. He's getting hysterical. We've got to go with him. I need you to watch the bastard. Just follow. Maybe we lost a million with his assistant but we're not going to lose any more. Get here as soon as possible , wait outside the bank and then follow me and the banker wanker all the way. Keep your usual eagle eye open for trouble. For Christ's sake hurry. You've got to make it within 20 minutes."

Vuk sighed. He was thinking about Amparo. What a day! He hadn't even had time to call her since the aborted lunch the day before. He'd call her now. Make or break. Ask her to join him in Geneva. Tell her he had to go on a business trip that evening. She might just accept, if not he would catch her later.

His thoughts jolted back to Thomas. He'd managed to prevent him going back to his flat. Now what? He'd have to eliminate him today. He drove to the bank, parked outside and went up to the 5th floor. Solange greeted him and he extended his hand and smiled.

"Hello, Solange. I'm going to get a permanent job with you, I think. Make life easier. Seriously, sorry to bother you yet again. I just need to see Lucas two minutes."

Solange simpered a bit. She found this huge man irresistible. She even had fantasies about his massive frame on top of her and his doubtless huge member throbbing and thrusting inside her. She pulled herself together.

"Oh, Mr Havel, he left a few minutes ago. But he said he would be back to pick up something before getting his plane to Zurich. He won't be long."

Vuk was momentarily taken aback but collected his wits. "Oh, Zurich. Yeah, he told me over the phone. But I thought his flight was later. Oh well, no harm done, I'll accompany him to the airport, it'll be my pleasure. No, come to think of it, tell him I'll wait for him in the main bar at the airport – I'm double-parked downstairs. Don't want my poor car getting towed away." He winked at her, applying a thick layer of masculine charm.

Solange blushed and felt the spreading damp in her pants. Vuk smelled her excitement and attraction, pushing home his advantage. "Oh, er, Solange, would you, I mean, er, do you think you might accept an invitation to dinner? From me, that is?" Fuck the little bitch, he thought. That's what she wanted.

Solange looked demurely at her feet, pressed her finger to her lips and wrote her telephone number down on a piece of paper. Vuk slipped it into his pocket.

As he took the lift down to the ground floor his brain worked furiously. He'd got everything sorted now in his mind, in one go............get the cash, kill Lucas, kill Thomas.....Christ he was enjoying himself. Action, that was what had been missing from his life on the Côte d'Azur. The Cannes incident had been fun mind you. Momentarily he even forgot Amparo.

# FLIGHT

AS SOON AS HE HAD FINISHED his little personal synopsis of priorities Lucas had somehow shaken off the remainder of his alcoholic sloth and moved quickly. Luck was on his side. Both Amra and George were in the flat when he called. He told them to wake up Chloé, not ask any questions because he was sure they knew most of the answers, and pack bare necessities. He told them they were leaving immediately.

"Come on, Lucas, what are you trying to do? Let's not be so melodramatic . . . "

"Shut the fuck up, George. Do as I say. If we don't move out now, I swear to you we'll all get blown away. Ask Amra. She knows why. Don't try to be clever, or reasonable, or anything. For once, just do as I say. The taxi will be downstairs in ten minutes. Get all the passports together." He hung up.

True to his word, Lucas arrived within ten minutes. Chloé looked shocked and frightened, Amra glacially calm and George was tight-lipped and nervous. After Lucas' phone-call, Amra had revealed to George Havel's true identity. They agreed to say nothing to Chloé for the moment.

Lucas arrived at the front door, red faced and panting. "Are you ready? Got everything........?"

George interrupted him:

"Lucas, listen. If I understand things properly, this Racik bastard could be anywhere right now. He might be downstairs, who knows. Why not send the taxi away and I'll ferry you all down to the port one by one on the motorbike? We can leave by the back entrance to the garage and we'll have helmets. No-one would be able to recognise us."

Lucas scratched his head. Decisions, decisions. Jesus. Then his mind cleared again. "No, I've got to pick up some stuff at the bank. It'll take a few minutes. But I need the taxi."

There was obviously no time for arguments. George quickly agreed. "OK, then I'll leave with Amra on the bike and follow you. That way we can keep an eye on you. What the hell do you want in the bank?"

Lucas paused before replying. "Let's say it's something even more important than our passports." Instead of the habitual conspiratorial wink which accompanied Lucas' rare admissions, George received a stubborn and resolute scowl. He stared back at his brother.

"Jesus, you must be desperate."

"This is desperate, George. I'm sorry, it's my fault, I should have listened to you. And now you're in the shit as much as me. Racik wouldn't hesitate to use you as a bargaining chip. Now, are you coming or do you want to wait 'till he walks up the fucking stairs and chews us all to pieces?"

Chloé had been listening to all of this, aghast. "What have you done? What have you done, chéri?"

"I'll tell you calmly and quietly when we're sitting on the beach in Corsica, darling."

Chloé pouted and shut up. She took Lucas' hand. With that one simple gesture of loyalty, she stole his heart forever. He felt like crying and quickly pulled himself together. With everything else going on, any more emotion and he'd have a heart attack.

Chloé had one bag over her shoulder with their passports and some money, a cheque-book, some make-up and clean underwear.

Lucas had two large empty suitcases which he carried, one in his hand and the other under his arm. His other hand dragged Chloé downstairs to the taxi.

Amra and George already had their helmets on and each carried a small rucksack. Amra's was heavy. Faruk's revolver and hand-grenade nestled inside, wrapped in a small towel. This was as good a time as any for a showdown, she reflected. If there was a showdown. If there wasn't, she would say goodbye at the port and finish her business with Racik on her own.

Things were coming together faster than she had expected and in a completely different manner. Everything had kaleidoscoped within a period of 48 hours. She stared grimly at the mobile telephone she had clutched in her hand and thought of the message Vuk had left her ........he was leaving that very day on a business trip.......he had to tell her something.......it wasn't easy and he'd never said this to anyone in his life........he was in love with her.........would she please join him.....he was driving to Geneva..........he could pick her up at Geneva airport in two days........please Amparo, please.....

She smiled. Talk about poetic justice: murdering the loved ones of others and then being murdered by the one you loved. Her thoughts were interrupted by George who pulled her roughly down the stairs to the garage.

# LEAVING TOGETHER

%

BY THE TIME LUCAS walked into the bank, carrying two suitcases, it was 12.15h. Many of the staff had already gone for lunch, but the cashier was waiting with Solange to open the vault. Vuk waited downstairs, parked behind a lorry, but with a narrow angle of vision to the building.

He tapped the steering wheel impatiently, alert and poised like a cat. His mind was working furiously. The suitcases meant only one thing. Perfect: 4 million dollars already in the boot of the Audi, 9 million dollars more which Lucas would kindly bring down. He'd work out what to do about the money in Liechtenstein.

The instinct which had saved him from years of danger in the minefields and trenches of Yugoslavia told him now he had to scarper. Take off out of Nice, out of France. Disappear for at least a year. He'd scare the shit out of Lucas, maybe not kill him after all, and come back later for the remainder of the money.

Thomas? Of course. Vuk knew how he was going to frighten Lucas enough for him not to try to steal his money a second time. He'd execute Thomas in front of Lucas and his girlfriend. He glanced in his rear-view mirror. Thomas was there, parked 75 metres further down the Avenue de Verdun. Thomas flashed his lights. Lucas staggered out of the bank under the weight of the two suitcases. Vuk walked calmly up to him and slapped him on the back, in full view of Chloé and the taxi.

"Smile, Lucas, smile now and you'll be all right. Smile, drop the suitcases and shake hands."

Lucas achieved a ghostly imitation of a smile, more akin to the expression on a man's face preparing to be violently sick. He slowly lowered the suitcases and wondered, not for the first time in these last few days, if he was going to shit in his pants. The light glimmered in Vuk's eyes and he felt the terror stiffening his joints.

"Now, we're going to play this very friendly," continued Vuk, with a huge grin on his face. God, this was fun. What a pathetic spectacle Lucas made. "I'm going to pay the taxi and tell your charming little slut that your old buddy, Josef, is taking you in his car. Got it? Otherwise, slut is going to have a fucking great hole in her head."

Vuk grinned even more widely and slapped Lucas on the back again. He waved socially at Chloé who, still ignorant of his identity, waved shyly back at the huge, handsome man.

Lucas watched as Vuk walked calmly up to the taxi, paid the driver and helped Chloé out of the back onto the pavement.

"Bonjour, Mademoiselle, I'm taking over from the taxi. The very least a friend of Lucas can do. No luggage? Oh, of course, Lucas has the suitcases." Vuk let out a crude and insinuating laugh and took Chloé by the arm. Lucas followed helplessly in their wake. When they reached his Audi, Vuk opened the boot and took the suitcases, placing them with mock care in the boot and giving each one a little pat. Chloé started to look puzzled, then stiffened, only now aware that something was very wrong.

She started crying .

"I tell you what, Lucas. You always said you would like to drive an Audi. You take the keys and I'll sit in the back with the slut."

He pushed Chloé roughly into the back and dangled the keys mockingly in front of Lucas' face, who tried, and failed, to look reassuringly at Chloé and did as he was told.

# TERMINUS

THE ARBITRARY HAND of fate that had pulled everyone into Nice at the same time now seemed to be pushing them all to leave at the same time, creating an inauspicious bottleneck from which only some, or one, would emerge.

Vuk was still ruminating backwards and forwards about whether or not to kill Lucas after all and track down Jérôme at a later date to get access to the safe in Baransteitbank from him. The problem was would it be left there for long once Jérôme knew that Lucas was dead? And what about Thomas? He would have to be disposed of first, whatever happened. Improvise. He'd get it right.

"Just keep driving, Lucas. Take the Moyenne Corniche. Then the Grande. We're going to take the back road to Italy and then decide what to do with you and slut. You've been a naughty boy, Lucas."

Vuk looked at Chloé and placed a hand on her thigh. She tried to pull it off and wriggle away but it was like an iron clamp and she was already jammed against the car door.

"What about you, slut? You look as if you might appreciate something I've got waiting for you." He took her hand and placed it on his genitals. Chloé froze in horror as she felt his penis hardening and started crying again.

"Tell him to stop, Lucas! Please tell him to stop!"

Lucas started to shout. "For God's sake, Josef, leave her out of this! Let her go!"

He suddenly felt his head rammed against the car window as Vuk pressed his revolver hard into his right temple.

"Shut the fuck up, you runt!" Vuk grinned savagely at Chloé and pulled her skirt up to her panties. He took his erect prick out of his trousers and ripped the panties apart. Then he forced her round to face the car window and pulled her hips round so that her buttocks were against him.

"Nice bit of arse, Lucas. You've been doing all right for yourself. Do you like fucking her Lucas? Or is that a bit vulgar for private bankers? Maybe you just make polite conversation over some herbal tea before going to bed. Tell you what, I'm going to fuck her and when I've finished I'll hand her over to you and you can take over......get my meaning Mister smartarse Private fucking banker..........you do spell that with a 'b' don't you Lucas?"

Chloe started screaming and immediately received a powerful blow from Vuk's massive hand. Her head jolted back and she lost consciousness.

Lucas felt the tears rolling down his cheeks. He had to do something. Anything would be better than this. He started the climb up the Moyenne Corniche and wondered just where he would crash the car. It was their only chance.

Within a few minutes he turned left onto the drop road leading to the Grande Corniche. He thought of Cary Grant and Grace Kelly, for a fleeting stupid second, as he pictured them driving along the same road.

Vuk fondled Chloé's buttocks and stroked her neck with the barrel of his revolver. He stared at his unruly organ and decided that his fun would have to wait. No point in fucking the woman when she was out for the count anyway. He wanted to hurt her, see the panic and suffering in her eyes. Make sure Lucas was watching.

"Lucas, turn off to the left. Drive up that track until I tell you to stop. I'm going to check the suitcases, Lucas. Hope the full 9 million is there. I'm not leaving any in your stupid bank."

Lucas swore to himself. It was the exact spot where he had been going to ram the car into a tree. Involuntarily he had slowed down when Vuk had spoken and now the car didn't have the impetus to cause more than a nasty shock.

The track was barely more than a rock-strewn path and the car rocked badly, the chassis frequently scraping the ground and the sides scratched by overhanging branches. Vuk was talking into the mobile.

"Thomas, did you see us turn off?" Pause. "Good. Just follow us and join me and my friends when we stop. One of us is going to cover them and the other is going to count the cash in the suitcases. One centime less than 9 million and I want you to do to our bank manager and his slut what you did to those guys in the garage." Pause. "The garage in Avar, you idiot." Pause. "See you in a minute." He wiggled his tongue foully at Chloé who was just coming round.

Thomas narrowed his eyes. This was probably the moment. While checking the cash he would leave his gun on the roof of the car in full sight of Vuk who would think he was unarmed. As soon as Vuk turned his back, he would pull out the gun he kept strapped to his leg. Corny, but effective. He followed the cloud of dust up the side of the deserted hillside. He allowed himself one look to the right over the Mediterranean, only a few kilometres away and a few hundred metres lower but blurred by the afternoon haze.

He saw a clearing ahead, some 700 metres from the road and, parked in the shade under the branches of two large oaks, was Vuk's Audi. Lucas and Chloé were seated inside and Vuk stood outside, casually chucking the car-keys up in the air and catching them as they fell. His revolver was tucked in the front of his trousers. Thomas contemplated him as he approached. All that muscle and bulk, shortly to be rendered lifeless by one carefully aimed bullet.

He pulled up next to Vuk's car and got out, expressionless as usual. "So, what's up, Vuk? Has our little friend been greedy? Has he been dishonest?"

Vuk smiled, totally relaxed. "He's got a couple of suitcases, which I haven't had time to open yet. But we know what's in them, don't we, Lucas?" He put his hand through the open window of the car and pulled Lucas' head back by his hair and then rammed it forward onto the steering wheel. Blood immediately spurted out of Lucas' broken nose. Chloé screamed. Vuk turned on her.

"Shut up, slut, or I'll have to cut your vocal chords. Which is what should be done to all you bitches anyway. At birth." Chloé cowered back into the corner of the car while Lucas tried to muster his wits and staunch the flow of blood with his Gucci tie.

Vuk spoke to Thomas. "Here are the keys to the boot. I want you to open the suitcases and count the money. Our private banker is going to watch you as you do it, together with his slut and, when you've finished, I want you to punish them, Thomas. Just like you did the last ones who tried to cheat. Then we get out of this fucking place. We're going to set up shop somewhere else."

Vuk pulled Lucas out of the car and stood him next to the back of it. Then he opened the back door and put his massive hand round Chloé's neck. "Come on, slut, come and take a look at all that money you might have been able to spend. Take a good look, slut, 'cos it's the last time you're going to see it."

Lucas and Chloé stood together, their arms around each other, each trying, despite their panic and bewilderment, to give some comfort to the other.

"Hey, Lucas, looks like slut really loves you. I find that so sweet. But when I've finished with her she's going to love me. She's going to find out what a real man is like, Lucas."

Lucas' jaws tightened and he felt the hot prickle of fury mounting in his body. He panted slightly and the adrenalin made his heart beat faster.

Thomas placed his revolver casually on the roof of the car and inserted the key into the boot lock. He lifted the lid and peered inside. He saw the suitcases first and was about to pull them out when he saw the rucksack he'd hidden in his flat. Too late. He knew Vuk would have his revolver trained on him. He wouldn't even be able to reach for the gun strapped to his leg. He slowly straightened and turned his head towards Vuk.

As he did so he found that it was true: your whole life really did flash in front of you a few seconds before you died. He saw the sunlight through the upper branches of the oak tree. He felt the warmth and for the first and last time in his life caught a momentary glimpse of something beautiful.

"You know, Thomas, I really couldn't give a stuff. But I saved your life in Bosnia. You remember? The pigs were going to slit your throat. This is how you repay me."

One bullet shot into Thomas' stomach. He crumpled. Thomas clutched his abdomen and trembled in agony. Vuk looked him in the eyes for a few seconds. He wanted Lucas and Chloé to take it all in. Thomas' suffering was so acute he was obviously going to pass out.

"OK, Lucas. This is what happens to those who cheat me." He fired a second bullet into Thomas' head and tucked the revolver back into his trousers. Thomas' gun, left on the roof, was unloaded and thrown towards the bushes.

George and Amra witnessed the scene from behind some trees and thick undergrowth, some 70 metres away. George had followed Thomas at a considerable distance, taking care to keep behind other vehicles and avoid detection as far as possible. He had just seen the tail-end of Thomas' car turning up the track and had followed slowly, stopping often to check he could still hear the car's engine. The motorbike was making very little noise as it went up the track at barely 5 K.P.H.

When he had ascertained that Thomas' car had stopped, he pushed the bike into the trees, hid it behind a wild rhododendron bush and walked stealthily uphill with Amra on the side of the track, until the two cars became visible. They cut into the woods and approached from a different angle.

Only Amra had held George back when he saw his brother emerge from the car, covered in blood.

"He's OK. He's walking. He might have lost a couple of teeth or broken his nose, but that's all. Wait. We've got to work out how to get them both, Thomas and Vuk. For God's sake don't ruin everything. Either we stay out of sight or we all get killed, Lucas first. We won't stand a chance. Trust me George. Look". She showed him her revolver.

It was at this moment that they saw Vuk training his gun on Thomas.

"I think our problem has just been halved. What the fuck is going on? Whose side . . . ?" George stared, bemused.

They watched Thomas' execution. Amra narrowed her eyes. George felt the panic mounting in him to an almost uncontrollable level. He was again on the point of rushing forward, to try to save his brother.

Again, Amra calmed him. "George, do as I say. I'm going to get closer. If we do anything stupid now, we've all had it I tell you. George, George, I know it's your brother. We've got to get it right. Don't rush in there. I want you to stay here. I'm going to shoot him, I swear to you."

Before George could say or do anything more, Amra pressed her finger to her lips and then pulled the grenade out of her bag. She mimed how to prime it. "God knows what you can do with this. Just a last resort." She smiled. "Just don't throw it too close to me!"

She kissed him on the forehead and moved forward on her hands and knees. Within two minutes she had closed the gap between her and Vuk to 50 metres.

Still too far to risk a shot, she paused and listened to snatches of Vuk's monologue:

" . . . key to the safe . . . I'll be back . . . first I'm going to tie you to this tree . . . show you what a real man can do . . ."

Suddenly she heard a scream. Lucas literally went berserk, hysterically and furiously. He charged at Vuk and, with the strength of a madman, smashed his fist into his left eye and toppled him to the ground, tugging at his hair, panting and crying, flailing at the enormous man beneath him.

Vuk roared like a bull, taking seconds to recover from the surprise attack. He grabbed Lucas by the neck and struck him on the side of the head with his fist, throwing him to one side like a doll. He scrabbled around on the ground for his revolver, cursing in Serbian. He couldn't find it. He rubbed his wounded eye and stood up.

Chloé, holding the gun in both hands, was trembling and white. She pointed it at him, arms outstretched, terror and desperation on her face. The gun felt heavy.

"Give me that, you stupid bitch. Give it to me straight away or I'll break your neck. I'll break your boyfriend's neck."

Vuk kneeled down and jerked Lucas' head back to a horrifying angle. "One more millimetre and you'll hear it snap. Now give me the fucking gun."

Vuk watched Chloé, wide-eyed and motionless, the gun still held in her two hands, staring wildly past him. He looked round and saw a woman's figure, clad in black leather, wearing a motorcycle helmet.

This woman was as steady as a rock, fearless and resolute. She held a large, old-fashioned revolver and when she spoke, despite the nasal resonance of her voice inside the helmet, there was something familiar in the intonation and pitch.

He frowned and felt a prickle of fear. He lunged at Chloé, tackling her and grabbing for the revolver. He felt something slam into his back like a sledge-hammer. Chloé crawled away, choking with panic and Vuk watched her, helpless and winded by the bullet.

The helmeted woman approached. She kicked his revolver away towards the bushes and pointed her's at Vuk's head.

"Who are you?" asked Vuk. The woman didn't move, lowering the gun slightly. He saw her finger whitening on the trigger. The pain in his back was growing but he could stand it. The failure to understand was worse. He struggled frantically for words.

"Wait. What do you want, money? How about a million dollars? Cash. Who are you working for? Don't shoot me – I've come too far to be stopped now. Please, talk. Tell me what you want."

Amra stared down at the wounded man and fired a second shot into his left knee. Vuk screamed and roared with pain. He started to sweat and his face went white. Then he became silent, summoning all his strength. He continued panting, both hands round his knee, his back already rigid from the first shot.

Amra slowly lifted the visor of her helmet. He still couldn't see enough of her face. Then she took the helmet off completely and shook her hair out. Vuk stared in blank, uncomprehending shock.

This was impossible. Nothing could be worse. A nightmare. It had to be.

"You . . . you . . . what is this?" All of a sudden he felt small and helpless. "I love you Amparo. I love you. Please don't do this. You don't understand. These people were going to steal everything I have in the world. I didn't know you knew them. Do you know them?" Despite his pain he suddenly felt ridiculous and he shut up.

Amra feigned surprise. "Don't tell me you really love me? Oh, if only I'd known, I thought your little message this morning was a joke."She fired another bullet into the same knee, shattering the hand that was holding it. "Now, tell me, Mr Racik, are you sure you really really love me? Sure you're not going to change your mind?"

Vuk spluttered, some blood trickling down the side of his mouth. He couldn't stop the tears of agony. "Are you mad?" he fell back into silence, his jaw clenched, his body shaking.

"Yeah, you might say that. Mad at you, Mr Vuk Racik. You killed all my family, Mr Racik. I'm the only one left. Try telling me something to calm me down." Her inner fury had partially evaporated as she looked at the fallen man as if he were a mad dog which needed to be put down.

George ran over and told her to stop it. He bent over Lucas, who was just coming round, his head in Chloé's lap. "We made it, Lucas. No need to worry now. We made it. Everything's OK.

Chloé's OK, I'm OK. Just take it easy . . ." Lucas looked up at him, nearly spoke, tried to focus on Chloé and then passed out again.

Events were interrupted by another two shots. These were accompanied by howls of agony. Amra was standing astride a crumpled Vuk, white with fury again, her eyes blazing.

"So this is the great Vuk? Quieten down now. Try and reflect on your revolting life, on all the suffering you have inflicted and then try and remember a village called Craljna. That was my village, where I was brought up. You came with your thugs and murdered my mother, my father and my sister. You would have raped and murdered me if you had seen me. That was a grave oversight Mr Racik and now you are going to pay. These are your last minutes on earth. Don't try and comfort yourself that there is an afterlife awaiting you. You have failed in every possible way. Your life has been like a plague, the black death and you are totally alone now. You are hated by everyone who knows of your existence. You imagined you could get away with what you have done? You are loathsome Racik, a coward, look at yourself crying and whimpering like a baby, begging for mercy. You make me want to vomit."

Vuk's face was almost paralyzed by his agony but his eyes were open and he stared at the ground.

"Tell me Racik, have you ever loved anyone? I bet you don't love me any more. What about your twin brother? Rumour has it that you love him a lot, that you spoil him, send him money so he doesn't have to work. Your identical twin, Racik, think about him as you die, maybe he will provide you some comfort. Think about him hard now."

Vuk frowned, seemingly puzzled, his eyes bulging. A momentary softening of his features.

"Now think about him even harder and imagine what I am going to do to him." Amra knelt down and stared her victim in the eyes. Her hoarse voice and wild face were terrifying. "I'm going to make him swallow red hot coal, imagine that. That is far worse than anything you ever inflicted. He's going to suffer so much your brother, think of his face twisted in agony as he rolls on the floor, think of the coal burning through his throat and stomach, the smoke from the burned flesh....."

Vuk groaned hideously and stared frantically back into Amra's eyes. "No, no, please no, anything but him, anything you want....."

Amra sat up and smiled maniacally at him. "Nothing doing Vuk Racik, and as you die now just remember your poor brother never really did anything that bad, he's going to suffer because of you."

Vuk's state of physical and mental torture reached its climax, Amra waved her revolver, waiting.

A full 30 seconds later there was a fourth and then a fifth shot. The howling stopped. Vuk lay dead beside Thomas, blood seeping from his two knees, his groin and a ghastly hole in the middle of his forehead.

Amra wiped the gun clean and placed it in Thomas' hand. Then she walked slowly to the bushes where she'd kicked Vuk's revolver and retrieved it. She wiped it on the same handkerchief and put it in Vuk's lifeless hand. She found Thomas' empty weapon, retrieved the magazine behind the car and put both in her bag.

"Well, it's going to look most unlikely, but the police are going to have to conclude that they killed each other. We'll leave a bundle of money on the ground. George, any ideas what we do with the rest?"

George stared at her, speechless. This was the woman he had gradually been falling in love with. She was terrifying.

"What do you think?" he croaked.

Amra picked up the rucksack out of the boot of the Audi, pulled out one of the parcels and ripped the brown paper off. Then she flung a million dollars onto Vuk's bloody carcass and said simply "Let's get out of here."

Nobody moved except Lucas who fluttered his eyelids and then groaned. George stayed rooted to the spot and Chloé stopped her rocking motion with Lucas' head which was cradled in her lap. Amra looked at them and tried to work out what to say to make them obey.

"Listen George, you too Chloé. I know all of this is a shock. Not for me, quite the contrary. You know my story George but you don't Chloé. I'll tell you later. But when I do tell it I don't want to be sitting in front of you in a prison cell. I want to be sitting peacefully somewhere on a yacht or in a beautiful house or........ anywhere , but I don't want to waste my life explaining all of this to the police first. Normal justice can't cope with all this. So let's just leave things as they are, take the money and then work out how to spend it. Otherwise I seriously think we'll end up in prison. Maybe for years. Particularly Lucas."

George looked at Chloe and nodded. Amra was right. Two choices: police, no money and the risk of some gross charge of being in cahoots with Lucas' money laundering or freedom and untold riches.

"Or just freedom, if you don't want the money," he added. Chloé blinked and stood up mechanically.

"OK George, you take your brother to hospital," said Amra. "Say he fell off the bike, anything you like. Come on, pour some water over his face." She looked in the Mercedes and found a half finished bottle of Evian and gave it to Chloé who poured it without thinking directly on to Lucas' head. It trickled down to his nose and he spluttered. George had to retain a nervous laugh as his brother sat up and stared with amazement at the mess of blood and water dripping on to his shirt.

"When they have sorted him out head back to the flat. Oh, George, if you take the rucksack with you, if you can manage it on the bike, Chloé and I will look after the suitcases. Won't we Chloe?" Amra gave Chloé an encouraging smile. Chloé nodded without saying a word and stroked Lucas' hair.

Lucas slowly stood up with Chloé's help and said "Let's go, George. I'm beginning to get fed up with all this. I want to go home." Then he smiled and George saw the older brother he loved and appreciated. "Enough is enough, I think we should get back." He stumbled and put his arm round Chloé's shoulder.

"Don't move for the moment," said George with his still croaky voice. "I'm going to get the bike. I'll be straight back. Chloé, try and get Amra's helmet on him."

Five minutes later Amra laughed as she watched Lucas stagger and then climb drunkenly on to the motorbike. George accelerated slowly and started his bumpy ride down the track, Lucas lolling from one side to another, the rucksack on his back.

Amra felt good. But the feeling of being in control and the elation of having accomplished what she wanted evaporated in a few seconds.

Her mind flicked back to her family and Faruk. She sat down. Chloé watched, speechless and uncomprehending as Amra started sobbing.

# POST TERMINUS

⁄⁄⁄

THREE HOURS LATER, all four were assembled in Lucas' flat. George had driven Lucas, appropriately, straight to the St. Georges clinic in Cimiez and waited (rucksack clamped tightly between his legs) while Lucas' nose was set in the emergency ward. Amra and Chloé had walked down to the nearest bus stop, having stuffed their handbags with 100 Dollar notes and hidden the suitcases under a pile of rocks some 700 metres equidistant from the road and Vuk's and Thomas' sprawled corpses. Amra had carefully wiped over the inside of Vuk's car.

At the last minute, while waiting for the bus, she apologised to Chloé, said she had changed her mind and that they should take the suitcases with them. She muttered something about the police and sniffer dogs and, after all they had been through it would be absurd to lose their compensation.

Despite their heavy baggage and dishevelled appearances the two women had attracted only a cursory glance from the bus driver and passengers and had descended from the bus at its final destination, the train station.

Both the suitcases and the rucksack were now on the floor in the middle of Lucas' living room.

George was the first to speak. "I hate to put the dampers on things when you're all so pleased but what the fuck do we do now? I mean, apart from having a bloody great drink."

Lucas managed a wan smile. "Have a bloody great drink, then another one, and celebrate being alive. I'm so sorry, I feel . . . well, kind of ashamed. I'm just a greedy old alcoholic who couldn't cope when things got out of hand." He poured himself a tumbler of Scotch by way of confirmation. "I could have got you all killed. In fact it's a miracle, a bloody miracle that any of us are still alive. I'm surprised you're even still talking to me."

Amra burst out laughing. "You're not quite such an arsehole as you imagine."

Lucas swallowed his drink gratefully and winced as he choked and coughed violently, making his face go red and his eyes water. "Jesus, Amra, where did you learn to speak such good English?"

"By frequenting you and George. But listen. Would you mind telling me, Lucas, what your biggest and most treasured financial project was until today? Don't bother, let me tell you, you were going to get a commission from Vuk for laundering his money. Bet that was all of 500,000 Dollars. Now let's do some simple arithmetic. Thanks to George, me and Chloé, without whose valuable help you would never have survived, let alone got your commissions, there is a total of . . . did you say 12 million Dollars? Well, if that were to be divided, just to take an example, into four equal shares . . . I mean there is you, Chloé, George and me, your $500,000 would look pretty pathetic wouldn't they?"

There was a moment of silence. All of them had been thinking about the money. Even George, who was beginning to get over the shock, found to his disgust that he was involuntarily focussing on the millions of dollars and how much he might get. Visions began to form in his mind of "George's", a gentleman's club with limited membership, leather armchairs, a snooker room, library, bar....

He snapped his mind back to everything they had gone through, how close they had been to death, the cinematic vividness of the violent dénouement on the Grande Corniche. Then he looked at his brother. He felt a sudden respect. Christ, Lucas had attacked Vuk, a man twice his size and four times his strength. He could have stayed still, paralysed by fear. But he hadn't. Lucas was not weak, he was just debilitated by alcohol and stress.

"Better make that five, Amra, you're forgetting Jérôme," said Lucas.

Chloé spoke for the first time. "Lucas, darling, if we're really one and the same, till death us do part . . ."

"Which it bloody well nearly did today, as a matter of fact," said Lucas, frowning as he guessed the direction of Chloé's thinking,

". . .then we can divide by four, can't we?" continued Chloé. " I think we can manage on 3 million Dollars. Don't forget we left 1 million on top of that Vuk brute. *Mon Dieu*, when I think what he was going to do to me. Anyway, let's settle for four shares. You and me together, Amra, George and Jérôme. After all Jérôme is just one in the calculation and he's married to Isabelle….. "

Lucas shook his head, George said he couldn't give a toss, Amra raised both hands to silence everyone and spoke again:

"Excuse me, you're all interrupting me. The other thing you achieved Lucas, is a thousand times more important than the money. Thanks to you I managed to realise my most precious dream. I killed Vuk Racik myself. That would normally be considered impossible. But I did it, thanks to you. You were the man who toppled him. I just had to walk up from behind and finish him off."

There was a moment's silence as Amra stopped talking, held up her glass and looked directly at Lucas. "Here's to you, Lucas, and you, George. You've looked after me, given me a bed to sleep in and put up with a stupid, depressed, obstinate, whining girl when you had much better things to do. And Chloé, you've been great. But then maybe you needed a bit of female company with these macho brothers around all the time. Anyway, you're my new family now. That's if you want me."

In his weakened state, pain and relief mixing with alcohol and confusion, Lucas let out a sob, but immediately controlled himself. The others pretended not to notice as he dabbed at his eyes and nose.

"Bloody dust, Chloé! I thought you were supposed to keep this place clean, that's what I pay you for." He slapped her, as usual on the behind with a disguised caress while Chloé feigned disapproval.

"Well, Amra, if you think about it, we both had the same enemy, but you're the one who got him, so here's to you and welcome to this crazy family. By the way, did I tell you where to send the rent you owe me?"

Laughter. At last, laughter. George was trying to say something but his silent paroxysms prevented him. Amra and the others followed his cue.

"Come on, George, spit it out."

George swallowed another half tumbler of JB. Then he managed to temporarily re-establish control.

"Lucas, tell us then, seriously, do you mind if Amra pays you in cash?"

Lucas laughed but then looked pensive. "You know, that may sound like a joke, but think about it. In actual fact, we have a mammoth money laundering problem facing us. How are we going to get this cash into a bank account?"

There was a moment of stunned silence, followed by further hilarity.

"Christ," said Lucas, "You're right I suppose. If anyone should know the answer to that question, I guess it's me....... but I just can't seem to see how to do it for myself. Seriously, does that mean I've finally gone down the drain? Alzheimers, or something?"

More drinks were poured. Silence slowly descended as everyone began to ponder the enormity of the situation.

Amra stood up and brushed the creases out of her skirt. "I've got to move. Faruk doesn't even know what has happened." She blew everyone a collective kiss and swung her handbag onto her shoulder.

Chloe said she would take a shower. The two brothers found themselves alone.

"Did I tell you about the Indian chief sitting in his wigwam?" George smiled. This was his joke. About time Lucas found himself on the receiving end. And it would do him good.

Lucas sat back with condescension. And relief. He felt the muscles in his shoulders relax. He sipped his drink and listened with satisfaction. The sillier the better.

Then he really started to feel better. He heaved a big sigh. Normality, glorious normality. George grinned at him.

# VIEW FROM A HOSPITAL BED

AMRA SPENT the rest of the day with Faruk. They held each others' hands, they cried and they started the long journey into the rest of their lives with at least the most important part of their past resolved by their act of courage and revenge. They realised now that ever since their witnessing of the horror, their sole ambition had been this act.

Faruk, still paralysed, had been obliged to live the whole action of the last week in his head. When Amra told him how she had personally executed their enemy he was initially shocked into silence but this gave way to a gasp of admiration.

"Amra, Amra, who would have guessed you would be the one to do this, I never thought .......... Well, I did think, but you're the sweetest, kindest girl in the world, my little sister, I mean nobody else would have guessed you were capable of this. Women, there is something about you that's a whole lot more dangerous than us men. We're little boys compared to you. Vuk Racik didn't stand a chance, did he?"

Amra laughed. "Beware the female of the species, she is by far the deadliest."

She was still incandescent with energy, anxious to define her next step. She couldn't see herself going back to Strasbourg. And she was rich now.

"Faruk, I'm going to see Saleh. I don't know why but I think he's going to help me, help us, to find the best way forward from here. He has some good ideas."

"You do that Amra. And stop thinking about me, stop worrying anyway. I have a feeling deep down in my soul that I'm going to recover fully. I feel incredibly good. Take some time off Amra, go and spoil yourself, go and spoil Saleh and his mates, go for a ride in the country, go and celebrate and rest and breathe and laugh.........."

"OK, if you don't see me for a couple of days it'll be your fault. But when I come back I want to see, at the very least, those toes wiggling."

It was Faruk's turn to laugh. "Take a look, lift the sheet." Amra obeyed and whooped with joy as she watched all five of the toes on his left foot perform a tiny curl.

%

George went to see Faruk the following morning. The change in the young man's face was so striking that George hesitated for a split second before being certain that he was in the right room.

Faruk grinned and they clasped hands. George looked into his eyes and saw something he did not quite understand. There was a quality of light and depth that defied description.

"You look amazing," he said feebly.

"Must be the vitamins they're giving me," replied Faruk. "And I'm sorry I can't return the compliment, George, but I think you should be taking some yourself. You look as if you've been washed up on the beach after a week of being tossed around in the wake of an ocean liner."

George chuckled at the metaphor. Quite apt really. The turmoil, the churning emotions, Vuk's flailing violence.

"Well, to be perfectly candid with you, things have been a bit tiresome of late." George knew that Faruk loved his understatements. "I mean I came down her for a bit of sun and restorative provençale peace as an antidote to London. And what do I get? Mixed up in a story which nobody would believe even if I were to tell it. Can't tell it to anyone anyway of course."

"Yeah, 'a bit tiresome' eh George? I reckon our respective guardian angels are pretty extenuated by now don't you? I think we'd better keep to the straight and narrow for a while and give them a rest."

"I was keeping to the straight and narrow for God's sake. What the hell would have happened if I'd been looking for trouble?"

Faruk gave him a wry look. "Aha, God again. I've been reading your *Brothers Karamazov.* You're a clever old devil George, but there is hope for you yet. Because if you have to use some eminent Russian intellectual to prop up your atheism it shows you're not sure of yourself. Anyway, I found exactly what you wanted me to read."

He handed the first volume over to George, opened at the presumed correct page. George looked down and nodded as he speed read the familiar words:

*"Answer me",* (said Ivan) *why are we meeting? To talk about my love for Katerina Ivanovna, about Dmitry and the old man? About life abroad? About Russia's fateful situation? About the Emperor Napoleon? No we must solve the everlasting questions, that is our concern......Believest thou or dost thou not believe? ...........Is there a God, is there immortality?*

*If God exists ......... this world of God's, I don't accept it, even though I know it exists, and I don't admit its validity in any way. ...........Even in the final moment of eternal harmony.......the soothing of all indignation, the redemption of all men's evildoings and of all the blood that has been shed by them.......I will not and do not want to accept it!"*

*"Will you explain why you don't accept the world?" Alyosha said.*

*"Of course..." Ivan smiled, for all the world like a meek boy. "I was going to speak to you of the suffering of mankind, but let us rather concentrate on the sufferings of children...........Children when they are children, until the age of seven for example, are terribly apart from other people; it is as though they were a different species with a different nature.............*

*"Where is this going?" Alyosha asked.*

*"I have a great, great many true stories about Russian children in my collection , Alyosha. Listen to just this one, and its not even the worst. The father and mother of a little five year old girl, 'most respectable and high ranking people, educated and of progressive views', conceived a hatred of her. Let me tell you, I once again positively assert that in many scions of mankind there is a curious property - the love of torturing children, but only children......... It is the very unprotected aspect of these creatures that tempts the torturers, the angelic trustfulness of the child which has nowhere to go and no one to turn to- this it is that excites the foul blood of the torturer........those progressively educated parents subjected that poor five year old girl to every torture one could think of. They beat her, flogged her, kicked her, themselves not knowing why, turned her whole body into a mass of bruises; at last they attained the highest degree of refinement: in the cold and freezing weather they locked her up for a whole night in the outside latrine because she did not ask to be relieved (as though a five year old child, sleeping its sound angelic sleep, could learn to ask to be relieved at such an age). What is more they smeared her eyes, cheeks and mouth with faeces, and it was the mother, the mother who did the compelling!*

*"And that mother was able to sleep, hearing at night the moans of the poor little child, locked up in the foul latrine. So now do you*

*understand, when a small creature that is not yet able to make sense of what is happening to it beats its hysterical breast in a foul latrine, in the dark and cold, with its tiny fists and wails with its bloody, meek, rancourless tears to 'dear father god' to protect it... now do you understand? The entire universe of knowledge is not worth the tears of that little child addressed to 'dear father God'.*

*"Tell me yourself directly, I challenge you, reply: imagine that you yourself are erecting the edifice of human fortune, that you are God, with the goal of, at the finale, making people happy, giving them peace and quiet, but that in order to do so it would be necessary and unavoidable to torture to death only one tiny little creature, that same little child that beat its breast with its little fist, and on its unavenged tears to found that edifice. Would you agree to be the architect on those conditions, tell me and tell me truly."*

*"No, I would not agree," Alyosha replied quietly.*

There was a moment's silence as George felt the impact of the words, strong and dismaying as ever. "OK, so what do you say to that, Faruk. Every time I read it I find it more irrefutable. God either doesn't exist or if he does he isn't the great beneficent and compassionate one we are taught to imagine."

Faruk concentrated. "All of that is powerful and shocking but while being as horrified as you by the tale I still manage to retain my faith. I'm not a fanatic George. You know me better than that and you've shared many a pint of beer with me so I'm not exactly a perfect example of any faith. I don't reject anybody or anything except what is evil, objectively evil to every religion under the sun, and I believe that all the great prophets, including Abraham, Moses, Jesus, and Mohammed teach in the name of God. It's as simple as that.

"There are rules to respect regarding honesty, charity, kindness to women and children, love and mercy.......everything.

"We are divided persons George. The human part rebels against God but our spirit, the other 'component' if you like, is with God. And so we have to fight to make the human part submit to the divine part while we are physically here on earth and alive. This is the battle, between base human nature and the divine self, that we must win.

"It's a holy war we have to wage with ourselves. You have to aspire to moving upwards George, not downwards to where our feeble and ignoble nature drags us.

"Now if you can understand that, you can understand that this terrible tale in *Brothers Karamazov* is one which should lead us on with even greater clarity to fight evil in the name of God, not one which provides us with a reason to renounce belief in his existence.

"What have I been doing for my family? I have been fighting evil George. Action, that is how you eliminate evil, example, not by turning the other cheek.

"For me God is hope, a sort of oxygen. And I can accept deep down that others find their oxygen through different sources and perceptions of God. That's not a problem. We need God like we need a mother and a father, someone from whom we came. We had to come from somewhere George. Even you!"

George interrupted. "There you go, Faruk, we need him so we invent him. And once we have each invented our own version of God, we appoint some holy men, make up some pious ritualistic crap and go to war to impose our God on others because he's the best one."

Faruk shook his head. "I'm not interested in polemical stuff about how religion generates oppression and is exploited to bamboozle the masses which is the next thing you are going to tell me. What I'm saying is that as long as things like this happen (things like those which happened to my family, those which happened to the little girl) it is only faith that can keep us going. Otherwise why bother? If it's inevitable, if there is nothing you can do, if the only thing you can say is 'If God existed he would never allow this,' if you just turn the other cheek, then you are doomed to porcine inertia and your spirit will cave in to your baser self and despite your elevated status as a 'human being' you will become no better than a beast."

"Jesus," said George, suddenly taken aback by Faruk's speech.

His blasphemous reaction accorded so perfectly with Faruk's caricature of him that both men laughed.

George drew in his breath to voice the objections that had been forming in his mind for the last ten minutes and his firm conviction that Faruk was a bit of a nutcase. But he changed his mind. Why try to argue with the beliefs of a man using his mean western rationality? Faruk was a peaceful man, not a terrorist and certainly not a religious fanatic. He just believed in God. And if he wanted to explain the justice meted out to Vuk not just in terms of straightforward revenge but also in terms of some elevation of his spirit, fair enough. He looked at him again.

Faruk appeared to be totally in harmony with himself and the world. His face was smooth , his brow unfurrowed, his eyes calm and rather beautiful. His mind, his heart, his faith, his actions all seemed to have meshed to create balance and synergy. Lying in bed in front of George was a person who seemed about as complete as one could ever hope to be. And he'd got there his own way.

And surely that was what it was all about? Eh, Alfie?

# EPILOGUE

VUK'S DEATH was initially a mystery to the local police. But Amra's friends, as soon as they discovered from her what had happened, published "his assassination" on "Balkan Website" as a victory for the Bosnian Muslims. The Serb propaganda machine snapped into action and claimed his demise was the result of the Serbian military police's active intervention to punish and put down a traitor, a man who, after all, was not 100% Serbian. He had turned his back on the war because he was a coward. He was an example of what would happen to anyone who deserted.

"Nice Matin", the local newspaper, made a fuss for a few days, speculating about the implications. Was this the presage of a new wave of Eastern European mafia, installing itself on a Côte d'Azur already rotten with corruption? Who really believed that the two unidentified men had killed each other? If there was another party involved, why did it leave a million Dollars littered over the corpses? What was the connection with the disappearance of a prostitute on the same night as the death of three men in Cannes?

Lucas returned to the bank the day after the traumatic events on the Grande Corniche. He told Solange he'd missed the plane to Zurich and, having returned to pick up his car, had had an accident on the way to the bank. He smashed in the front of his beloved Jaguar to prove it with the help of George, who chose the most appropriate wall in the underground garage belonging to Lucas' block of apartments.

In the instinctive way that people steer back to normality and routine the strange behaviour of Lucas over the last few weeks was forgotten by his colleagues and they discovered an even better version of the old Lucas they had all so liked and respected.

Lucas stopped drinking for a full month as his nose recovered and he laid his plans with Jérôme. The latter's stay in Vintimiglia hospital was limited to ten days, after which he spent a month in a "Centre de Récupération" in the mountains near Auron, the skiing resort above Nice. The police never linked Jérôme's shooting to the events on the Grande Corniche and his name was never mentioned in the papers.

Bizarrely, now that the cash was theirs, the whole question of how to launder it to legitimate bank accounts became more fraught. They even wondered what they would do if and when they did manage to officialise it. In the end, they and their wives (Lucas married Chloé six weeks after the shoot-out) carried out small exchange operations in different banks and *agents de change* in Nice, Cannes and Antibes to supply themselves with generous amounts of pocket-money in local currency.

Their official salaries were saved and used to justify loans from local banks to buy new homes in Châteauneuf de Grasse. A large part of the unofficial price was settled in cash. Lucas bought a magnificent villa with five bedrooms and 7,000 square metres of land, a swimming pool and mature fruit trees. During weekends, he did indeed watch Chloé's neat little buttocks swaying with the movement of her hips as she picked the fruit and pruned the rose bushes. And he drank his bottle of Rosé every day but never touched spirits again. This was, he claimed, a sensible compromise. "Balance," he philosophised, the most important word in the dictionary with the secret to a happy life contained in it.

Jérôme bought the villa next to his "patron". It was similar, although more modern, to that of Lucas. He installed a wine cellar for Lucas, as a belated wedding present. Behind the racks of wine, perfectly dissimulated, he constructed an artificial wall. Behind this, the two men kept their vast stack of cash.

Isabelle and Chloé became, as Lucas put it, bosom friends. Isabelle held Chloé's hand when she gave birth to her first child.

And what about the other protagonist in this tale of money, murder and mayhem? Well, I know it's a bit late, but it's me. I'm George, you see. That's how I know so much. I've waited a few years to write all this down and I've changed a few names. My own, for a start - my surname, that is - not my first name. I really am George but Lucas isn't Lucas and Amra isn't Amra so all similarities etc. are purely coincidental.

But I'm bloody rich and so is my dear older brother, who has made me an uncle thrice over.

When I embarked on writing this I wanted to put down everything as it happened. The "uneasy mixture of violence, knockabout humour and dicey politics" as one of my erudite friends described this tale seems to me a fair comment but not a fair criticism: since when was real life totally balanced and coherent? Every day, for me, seems to have it's own mixture of contradictions, pleasure and pain, achievement and frustration. And even the odd swing from the ridiculous to the sublime. Like my conversation with Faruk, pondering the imponderable.

Let's get back to me and Amra. I bet you wanted a lot of romance there, didn't you? Well, let's put it this way. I really went for Amra. I still think she is one of the most beautiful women I've ever met. And I left out a few details about what happened in Lucas' flat. We both needed a lot of comforting, and that's what we did. Comfort each other. All right, we were at it like rabbits from the outset but there was no point in putting that into the story because it had nothing to do with the main plot. Also, it would have been difficult to mention it without casting the mourning Amra in the wrong light.

Anyway, after Amra began to show her teeth, I got frightened. You know, it's all very well being with a beautiful girl, but if you know she's bent on murdering someone, never mind whom, it kind of puts you off. There you are, tenderly making love, and you suddenly realise she's thinking of which one of Vuk's testicles she's going to cut off first. Sort of thing a chap can do without. I never thought she'd fly off the handle with me and suddenly cut my throat or anything. After all, she was and is part of the family now. But she'd been through things which didn't bear thinking about and that made her different and, ultimately, unpredictable.

But, dear Amra, if by any chance you read this and, of course, you won't fail to recognise yourself and all of us, please understand that you scared the shit out of me. You didn't want to stay and settle down with me anyway. You were off like a flash with that Saleh bloke, weren't you, investing all your money in the Bosnian cause? You'll probably be made into a Saint by the Bosnian Muslims some day. Or whatever the equivalent is.

And Faruk? Dear old Faruk. Well, he's my second brother like we agreed in the hospital. You know, events were so chaotic and traumatic towards the end that none of us, not even Amra, had time to even think about Faruk on the day. Mind you it wasn't as if we had abandoned him, it was just during that fateful day when we forgot about him and concentrated on surviving and killing the beast.

Faruk symbolises the happy ending to this part of my story more than anything else or anybody else. The end of Vuk released him from the captivity of his hatred. He found a new spiritual level of being.......Oh dear, I don't like this sort of observation, it makes me feel a bit embarrassed. Let's just say he emerged from that hospital a different man.

Somehow the whole epic voyage concorded with what God was telling him. Cleansing of his body and soul by purging himself and the world of the ultimate bastard. It didn't matter that it was Amra who pulled the trigger. It was all thanks to him that revenge was accomplished and the world was a cleaner place. So he studied and became a scholar and a holy man. How else can I put it? And he remains my spiritual brother and we see each other all the time. One way or another we all stayed on the Côte d'Azur you see, apart from Amra, as explained above.

Oh, and he got back the use of his legs. He always said he would. A simple matter of faith. He also got some of the money (in case you were wondering).

Just for the record, I kept that telephone number. Which telephone number? Go back to page 32 and you'll remember.

Well, she remembered me and was already on her way to the Côte d'Azur. I picked her up at the airport on Faruk's motorbike. She was tickled pink and still is to this day. I'm really sorry to make this sound even more like a happy ending but it's not my fault if the baddies got it in the neck and the goodies all seemed to live in peace and inner harmony ever after.

But did they, or rather, will they?

There's just one loose end, isn't there? Have you spotted it? Have you been paying attention? The money in the safe in Liechtenstein. That's a whole story in itself. I didn't get any of it and neither did Lucas or Jérôme. Rather than tell you now, I'll keep it up my sleeve and maybe write a second tome. Because the bloke who got it is really going to get it. In the neck. I'm no Vuk

Racik but I will not have people taking what is not rightfully theirs. Which leads me on to another loose end.

A loose end that's not in the story so much as in my mind which means in my life and which is in the mind and life of Lucas too.

Tainted money, that's what it is all about isn't it? Why do I get that feeling of dissatisfaction when I read back what I've put down on paper? Maybe you have to write things down before you can see them objectively. There was a lot of celebration and fun after the appalling session on the "Grande Corniche", partly thanks to the feeling of new found affluence but mainly due to the incredible feeling of release from the shackles of Vuk's presence and the fact that us amateurs had given him his comeuppance.....well, Amra did it really, but it was nevertheless a collective effort. And the euphoria lasted for a while.

But deep in our subconscious was the fact that we were living off the spoils of a murderous bloodthirsty bastard whom, well, we had in turn murdered....OK killed in self defence. Even if we hadn't killed him it still didn't change the fact that we were sitting on a pile of evil loot. All that stuff about money being odourless and morally exempt. It's not true.

At the very best of times, I  mean even when the money is clean, I don't reckon there is a great deal it can do for you. It can't buy you love and it can't really buy peace of mind, apart from some vague feeling of material security which in turn can lead to a sort of apathy.

I think a lot about Nath. She loves me OK but maybe the fun we have with my money isn't for real and maybe it makes her love me more, if you see what I mean, than she would do otherwise. So maybe part of her love is based on the wrong assumptions. And that makes me think I'm not worthy of it, that I'm conning her.

She looks at me with those adoring eyes, trusting me and thinking I'm the best and most noble thing since King Arthur.

The truth is I fucked off with nearly $3,000,000 of dirty money, literally still splattered with blood. And Nath thinks I won some on the lottery and then went on a Dostoevskian splurge at the casino. She has no idea how much I've got.

I feel bad about that and I feel bad about my brother. In fact I observe him with despair because he's much more troubled by the whole affair than I would have imagined possible. I think he was traumatised in some way. "He never touched spirits again" was, as the years went by, a euphemism for "he got pissed on wine instead".

He took to sitting for hours in his beloved cellar with a bottle and a glass on the barrel he used as a table, sipping away until he dozed off, pissed out of his mind. Chloé told me about it and how increasingly she brought up the children on her own. That said, the only little clue I will give you about my next and putative tome is that, à propos of Lucas , one of the themes might best be called "renaissance."

You know how life is a process of evolution? You have to move vertically and not horizontally. Faruk said a few wise words about that. Sometimes you make a downwards vertical movement ( you slip and go arse over tit as Lucas would put it) and then the graph picks up again.

Well I'm leaving you during one of those dips or slips to tell you the truth. I don't feel free in my head. I've got to do something about the money. I don't want anything that it's bought me. You remember Amra said we could either be broke and in prison or rich and free? We found that an overpowering argument for never telling anyone, let alone the police. But now I feel rich and in prison and I'd rather be broke and free. I feel better now that I've admitted as much.

I'd rather be back working my arse off in the "Yacht". I can't stand it anymore, this feeling of uncleanliness. As I write these words I know I've got to get rid of it all. That is going to be my freedom, my sort of spiritual release. My Jihad. You know, when you see someone as clean as Faruk you can't just stay where you are. Unfinished, unaccomplished, unclean because of apathy and unambitious contentment with the banal and venal aspirations of a mediocre life. Heavy stuff. Sorry.

I can see Nath coming in from the garden side of our house. She's carrying her roller blades bless her little heart. She is going to be the first person to know.

"Nath".

"Oui chèrie?"

"Come here darling. I've got a lot of things I want to tell you about. And I want to know something: if you had $3.000.000 which you couldn't keep, which you had to give away, what would you do with it?"

THE END

## NOTES/REMARKS/REFERENCES

Page 14 & others on Alcoholism Adapted from: Diagnostic and Statistical Manual of Mental Disorders. Vol. IV American Psychiatric Association. 1994

Page 74 & others inspired by a review: Mary L. Gavin, MD Date reviewed: February 2006

Coming up next: **"Riviera Renaissance"**

Lucas' version of events(faithfully recounted by George) casts a different light on all the characters, corrects a few of George's "misconceptions" and picks up the story from where his brother left off with his epilogue.

The elder brother takes us closer to the real taste and smell of life on the Côte d'Azur and recounts the tortuous strategy and sometimes extreme action behind the attempt to get the remaining cash back from Liechtenstein.

The sudden appearance of Vuk's vengeful and greedy twin brother does nothing to simplify the situation!